"Ask me," April said jolting through her.

Patrick's eyes jerked to hers. "What?"

"Ask me out."

"April—"

"Nothing fancy," she said, hoping she didn't sound desperate. Because she wasn't. Really. "Dinner at Emerson's. Maybe a movie. If things work out…" Her heart thumped against her sternum. "Maybe a good-night kiss at the end."

Oh, dear. Poor baby actually flinched. And not, she didn't think, because he found the idea appalling. Strange, and wonderful, the feeling of power that gave her. Frowning though he was.

"I thought I made it clear—"

"What's clear," she said with remarkable calm, considering, "is that there's something humming between us. Agreed?"

Dear Reader,

I was just starting to develop this story when I started watching Season 13 of *Dancing with the Stars*. And within minutes of "meeting" J. R. Martinez, the severely burned Iraq War vet who went on to win the coveted mirror ball trophy, I had my hero. J.R.'s drive to push himself past what some might have seen as limitations—and his undeniable sex appeal as a result—was a true joy to watch. And served as an incredible inspiration for my own Patrick Shaughnessy.

Not that Patrick's quite in the same place J.R. is, attitude-wise. At least not when his story starts. But that's where cute little April Ross comes in. Because the brand-new innkeeper is determined to smack some sense into Patrick. To make him accept that her heart is far bigger than the three acres she's hired him to landscape, big enough to love him and his little girl both. Add to that a huge Irish-American family, equally determined to see their Patrick return to a normal life after the combat injury that's left him scarred, both physically and emotionally, and you have a story about giving and loving and never giving up that's just perfect for the holiday season.

Enjoy!

Karen Templeton

A GIFT FOR
ALL SEASONS

KAREN TEMPLETON

HARLEQUIN®
entertain, enrich, inspire™

If you purchased this book without a cover you should be aware that this book is stolen property. It was reported as "unsold and destroyed" to the publisher, and neither the author nor the publisher has received any payment for this "stripped book."

Recycling programs
for this product may
not exist in your area.

ISBN-13: 978-0-373-65705-6

A GIFT FOR ALL SEASONS

Copyright © 2012 by Karen Templeton-Berger

All rights reserved. Except for use in any review, the reproduction or utilization of this work in whole or in part in any form by any electronic, mechanical or other means, now known or hereafter invented, including xerography, photocopying and recording, or in any information storage or retrieval system, is forbidden without the written permission of the publisher, Harlequin Enterprises Limited, 225 Duncan Mill Road, Don Mills, Ontario M3B 3K9, Canada.

This is a work of fiction. Names, characters, places and incidents are either the product of the author's imagination or are used fictitiously, and any resemblance to actual persons, living or dead, business establishments, events or locales is entirely coincidental.

This edition published by arrangement with Harlequin Books S.A.

For questions and comments about the quality of this book, please contact us at CustomerService@Harlequin.com.

® and TM are trademarks of Harlequin Enterprises Limited or its corporate affiliates. Trademarks indicated with ® are registered in the United States Patent and Trademark Office, the Canadian Trade Marks Office and in other countries.

www.Harlequin.com

Printed in U.S.A.

Books by Karen Templeton

Harlequin Special Edition

§*Husband Under Construction* #2120
‡*Fortune's Cinderella* #2161
‡‡*The Doctor's Do-Over* #2211
‡‡*A Gift for All Seasons* #2223

Silhouette Special Edition

****Baby Steps* #1798
****The Prodigal Valentine* #1808
****Pride and Pregnancy* #1821
††*Dear Santa* #1864
††*Yours, Mine...or Ours?* #1876
††*Baby, I'm Yours* #1893
§*A Mother's Wish* #1916
§*Reining in the Rancher* #1948
††*From Friends to Forever* #1988
§*A Marriage-Minded Man* #1994
§*Welcome Home, Cowboy* #2054
§*Adding Up to Marriage* #2073

Harlequin Romantic Suspense

†*Plain-Jane Princess* #1096
†*Honky-Tonk Cinderella* #1120
What a Man's Gotta Do #1195
Saving Dr. Ryan #1207
Fathers and Other Strangers #1244
Staking His Claim #1267
♦*Everybody's Hero* #1328
♦*Swept Away* #1357
♦*A Husband's Watch* #1407

Yours Truly

*Wedding Daze
*Wedding Belle
**Wedding? Impossible!*

**Babies, Inc.
†How to Marry a Monarch
*Weddings, Inc.
♦The Men of Mayes County
††Guys and Daughters
§Wed in the West
‡The Fortunes of Texas:
 Whirlwind Romance
‡‡Summer Sisters

Other titles by this author
available in ebook format.

KAREN TEMPLETON

Since 1998, two-time RITA® Award winner and Waldenbooks bestselling author Karen Templeton has written more than thirty novels for Harlequin Books. A transplanted Easterner, she now lives in New Mexico with two hideously spoiled cats and whichever of her five sons happens to be in residence.

To Jessica Scott,
who took time out of her own writing schedule
to help me get the army details right.
At least, I hope I have.
Thanks, hon!

Chapter One

A weeper by nature, April Ross was the type to keep tissues at hand in case a coffee commercial took her by surprise. And, granted, the past several weeks had been an emotional roller coaster ride of reunions and massive renovations and reassessments of what she wanted from life. But to find herself nearly in tears—April dug in the only real designer purse she'd ever owned for one of those tissues and blew her little ice cube of a nose—over a bunch of *plants?*

Beyond pitiful.

Especially since she'd been the one who'd said, "What's the big deal? You go to a nursery, you pick out some trees, hire a couple dudes to stick 'em in the ground, done."

No wonder her cousins had rolled their eyes at her.

Now, huddled inside her thick cardigan against the bay wind shunting through the garden center, she turned on the heel of her riding boot and marched past a mess of pumpkins to the checkout area, where the bundled-up, gray-bearded black man behind the register released a soft chuckle.

"Somebody looks a little overwhelmed," he said in the relaxed Maryland shore drawl that immediately evoked memories of those childhood summers. "Not to mention half-frozen. So first off, step closer to the heater—go on, I'll wait—then tell me how I can help. I reckon I know pretty much everything about whatever's in stock. You got questions, you just go ahead and ask."

April's eyes welled again, both at his kindness and the lovely heat waves rippling from the nearby metal obelisk. "What I've got," she said as she removed her gloves, stretching her cramped fingers toward the heat, "is three acres of dirt and renovation mess that needs landscaping. By the middle of December, when my first guests arrive."

The man's eyebrows rose. "You the gal who's fixing up the Rinehart place?"

"That would be me." April tucked her wind-ravaged hair behind her ear, then extended her slightly warmer hand. "April Ross."

"Sam Howell. It's a real pleasure, young lady." Sam shook her hand, then crossed his arms high on his plaid-jacketed chest. "Three acres, you say—"

A child's excited squeal cut through their conversation. Grinning, Sam hustled from behind the counter a moment before a tiny, dark-haired blur slammed into him. After a fierce hug, the little girl backed up, all pink-cheeked adorableness in bright blue tights and a puffy purple jacket, and April's breath left her lungs.

"Daddy said I could pick out a punkin for Halloween!" she said, then planted a mittened hand against the front of the counter to awkwardly lift one glittery-sneakered foot. "An' I got new shoes! See?"

"Those are some rockin' shoes, Miss Lili. Your daddy pick 'em out for you?"

"Nope," she said with a vigorous head shake. "I choosed 'em all by myself. Mommy'll like 'em, huh?"

"Oh. Yeah. I'm sure she will…."

She turned her baby-toothed grin on April before letting her foot drop, twisting it this way and that to admire it. "Daddy says they're my *princess* shoes."

April laughed. "They certainly are," she said, as a toe-curling chuckle behind her sent the breath she'd barely pulled back into her lungs whooshing out all over again. Especially when the man—tallish, nicely shouldered, his face partially obscured by one of those silly hats with flaps covering his cheeks—scooped up his daughter and pretended to munch on her shoulder, making Lili giggle and sending April into a free fall.

Shoot. Shoot, shoot, shoot.

Automatically her left thumb went to her wedding rings, twisting them around until the diamonds dug into her skin, the sensation oddly soothing. Steadying. Yes, she should take them off already. But they made her feel…safe. Like the sweetest, most generous man she'd ever known was still watching over her, standing in the wings and cheering her on.

"Miss Ross," Sam said after the man untwined his little girl's hands from around his neck and set her down to go check out the pumpkins, "This here's Patrick Shaughnessy. And this young lady," he said with a wink in April's direction, "needs you bad."

So much for being cold. Heat swept across her face as she gaped at Sam, who—clearly enjoying her discomfiture—chuckled. "The Shaughnessys run one of the best landscaping outfits in the county."

"County, hell," Patrick said, turning just enough for

April to see his eyes, a bluer blue than hers, like lasers in a face still mostly hidden in the cap's shadows. Eyes that dimmed inexplicably when they met hers. "On the whole Eastern Shore." After a moment's hesitation, he offered his gloved hand, giving hers a quick shake before slugging it back into his jacket pocket. Canvas, no frills. Not exactly clean. His gaze shifted, presumably to keep an eye on his little girl, who meandered along the rows of pumpkins, like a finicky customer in a used-car lot, her face scrunched in concentration. "So I take it you need some work done?"

Deep breath. "I'd thought I could, you know, just buy some trees and things, hire someone to plant them. Until I got here and remembered I can't even grow a Chia Pet."

She thought his mouth might've twitched. "So how big's the lot?"

"Three acres or thereabouts." Another nippy breeze speared through the heater's warmth, making April wrap the sweater more tightly around her. She'd never been here in the fall, had no idea how brutal the damp cold could be. "I'm turning my grandmother's waterfront house back into an inn, so it needs to look halfway decent."

Another twitch preceded, "The Rinehart place?"

"Yes. How do—"

"Small town."

It was beginning to bug her that he kept his gaze averted. Especially since, as Sam had wandered out to help Lili select her pumpkin, the child was obviously okay. Patrick straightened, his arms crossed. "Got a budget?"

"Not really."

His eyes met hers and she felt like she'd been burned. All the way to her girly bits. So inappropriate, on so many levels—

"A couple hundred bucks?" he said, once more focused on his daughter. "A couple thousand…?"

"Oh. I see. Sorry, I honestly don't know. Even though... money won't be a problem."

The shock still hadn't completely faded, how well-off Clayton had left her. She'd had to have the lawyer reread the will three times, just to be sure she'd heard correctly. Clay's accompanying letter, however, she'd read herself.

"Yes, it's all yours, to do with however you like. As you can see, I kept my promise, too...."

"And yet," Patrick said, "you were thinking of handling the project yourself?"

She laughed. "I think it's pretty clear I wasn't *thinking* at all. So anyway—I'm almost always around, so... maybe sometime in the next week you could come out, take a look?"

"I'll have to check my schedule. But sure."

"Great. Here." April set her sunglasses and gloves on the counter to dig inside her purse for a business card, handing it to Patrick. He studied the card as though memorizing it, then pulled his own from his pocket.

"And here's ours—"

"Daddy! I found one!"

"Be right there, baby," he said, and April saw the tension slough from his posture...only to immediately reappear when his eyes once more glanced off hers before, with a curt nod, he walked away.

Odd duck, April thought, hiking up her shoulder bag as she tramped back out to her Lexus, a car that only five years ago she couldn't have dreamed would be hers. She'd no sooner slid behind the solid walnut wheel, however, when she realized she'd left her sunglasses on the counter. This was why, despite her much improved financial circumstances, she never paid more than ten bucks for a pair. Because she left them *everywhere*.

Shaking her head at herself, she trudged back to the nursery, plucking them—and her gloves, *sheesh*—off the counter as she heard Lili's musical, and irresistible, giggle again. Curiosity nudged her closer to the pumpkin display, where Patrick teased his daughter by pointing back and forth between two of the biggest pumpkins, saying, "This one. No, this one. No, *this* one. On second thought...I think it has to be this one...."

Fortunately, his back was to her so she could watch unobserved, finding some solace in the sweet exchange, even though it scraped her heart. He'd ditched that silly hat, so she could see his dark, barely there hair, almost a military cut—

He abruptly turned, his smile evaporating when he saw her, his gaze crystalizing into a challenge...

...in the midst of the puckered, discolored skin distorting the entire right side of his face.

And God help her, she gasped.

Mortified, she stumbled out of the nursery and across the graveled parking lot to lean against her car, trying to quell the nausea. Not because of his appearance, but because...

Oh, dear Lord—what had she *done*?

Expelling a harsh breath, April slowly turned around, her eyes stinging from the ruthless wind, her own tears, as several options presented themselves for consideration, the front-runner being to get in the car and drive to, say, Uruguay. Except...she couldn't. And only partly because she didn't have her passport with her. So she sucked in a deep breath, hitched her purse up again and started her wobbly-kneed trek back toward the nursery. Because those who didn't own their screwups were doomed to repeat them. Or something.

Sam chuckled when she walked into the office. "Now what'd you forget?"

"My good sense, apparently," April muttered, then craned her neck to see into the pumpkin patch. "Patrick still here?"

"Just left," Sam said, adding, when she frowned at him, "He was parked out back." At her deflated grunt, he said, "Need anything else?"

The name of another landscaper?

But since that would have required far more explanation than she was willing, or able, to give, she simply shook her head and returned to her car, hunched against the stupid wind and feeling like the worst person on the planet.

Yeah, that was about the reaction he expected, Patrick thought with the strange combination of annoyance and resignation that colored most of his experience these days. What he hadn't expected, he realized with an aftershock to his gut—not to mention other body parts further south— was *his* reaction to the cute little strawberry blonde. Which, while equally annoying, was anything but resigned.

A humorless grin stretched across his mouth. Guess he wasn't dead, after all. Or at least, his libido wasn't. Dumb as all hell, maybe, but not dead. Because, given how she'd recoiled, he was guessing the attraction wasn't exactly mutual. And even if it had been, those rocks adorning her ring finger may as well have been a force field against any wayward thoughts.

What he did have to consider, however, was whether to follow through on the job bid himself, or hand it off to his dad or one of his brothers. God knew he didn't need the temptation. Or the frustration. On the other hand, he

thought with another perverse grin, who was he to turn
down the opportunity to get up the gal's nose? Yeah, he
was one ugly sonuvabitch these days, but you know what?
The world was full of ugly sons of bitches, and the pretty
little April Rosses of the world could just get over it.

At the four-way stop that had come with the new de-
velopment south of St. Mary's Cove, Patrick laboriously
stretched the fingers of his right hand, the muscles finally
loosening after four years of physical therapy and innu-
merable surgeries. But at least he *had* his hand—

"Daddy?"

And at least his little girl had a father, pieced back together like a cross between Frankenstein's monster and
Dorothy's Scarecrow though he might have been. A lump
rising in his throat, he glanced in the rearview mirror at
the main reason he was still alive. Not that he wasn't grateful for the dozens of burn specialists and therapists and
psychologists who'd done the piecing. But whenever the
physical agony had tempted him to check out, he'd remember he had a baby who still needed him—even if her
mother didn't—and he'd somehow find the wherewithal
to make it through another day. And another. And one
more after that...

"C'n we give the punkin a face tonight?"

Patrick spared another glance for his daughter, out of
habit, taking care to avoid his reflection.

"Not yet, baby," he said, focusing again on the flat, field-
flanked road, the vista occasionally broken by a stand of
bare-limbed trees. "It's too early. If we do it now, it'll get
soft and sorry-looking by Halloween."

"When's that?"

"Five sleeps." He grinned in the mirror at her. To her,
he was just Daddy. What he looked like didn't matter, only
what he did. And what he'd done, since her mother left,

was make sure his daughter knew that he wasn't going anywhere, ever again. "Think you can wait that long?"

"I guess," she said on a dramatic sigh that reminded him all too much of Natalie, which in turn reminded him of Nat's brave-but-not expression after he was finally home for good, only to watch his marriage sputter and die. Not really a surprise, after what had happened. As opposed to his ex's decision to give Patrick full custody of their daughter, which had shocked the hell out of him.

"Where are we going?"

"Back to Grandma's."

The silence from the backseat was not a good sign. Patrick preempted the inevitable protest by saying, "Sorry, honey, I've gotta go back to work."

Among the many blessings of being one of seven kids, most of whom lived within a few blocks of each other, was that there was always someone to take care of Lili. In fact, his mother and oldest sister Frannie—at home with four of her offspring anyway—usually fought for the privilege. His child was in no danger of neglect. But over the past few months, Lilianna had become clingy and anxious whenever Patrick left. Especially since his ex's rare appearances only confused Lili, rather than reassured her.

He pulled into the driveway of his parents' compact, two-story house in St. Mary's. In her usual cold-weather attire of leggings, fisherman's sweater and fleece booties, a grinning Kate O'Hearn Shaughnessy greeted them at the front door, hauling her granddaughter into her thin arms. If you looked past the silver striping Ma's bangs and ponytail, the fine lines fanning out from her bright blue eyes, you could still see the little black-haired firecracker who'd rendered Joseph Shaughnessy mute the first time he laid eyes on her at some distant cousin's wedding forty years before. What his mother lacked in size, she more than made up for in spunk. And a death-ray glare known to bring grown men to tears.

"Go see Poppa," she said, bussing Lili's curls before setting her on her feet. "He's in the kitchen." Then she lifted that same no-nonsense gaze to Patrick he'd seen when he'd come out of his medically induced coma at Brooke Army Medical Center in San Antonio. If there'd been fear or worry, he imagined they'd been kicked to the curb before he'd even been airlifted from Landstuhl. "I made vegetable soup, you want some?"

"Sure."

Feeling like a burrowing gopher, Patrick followed her down the narrow, carpeted hall to the kitchen, careful not to let his wide shoulders unseat four decades' worth of baby pictures, school photos and wedding portraits plastering the beige walls. Like most of the houses in St. Mary's Cove proper, the house had been built in a time when people were smaller and needs simpler. That his parents had raised seven kids in the tiny foursquare was amazing in itself; that they'd never seen the need to upgrade to something bigger and better was a living testament to the "be content with what you have" philosophy they'd crammed down their kids' throats right along with that homemade vegetable soup.

Not that flat-screen TVs, cell phones and state-of-the-art laptops weren't in the mix with seventies furnishings and his grandmother's crocheted afghans. His parents weren't Luddites. But their penchant for shoehorning the new into the old had, over the years, shaped the little house into a vibrant, random collage of their lives.

This was also the home, the life, he'd returned to in order to heal, the safety and stability it represented restoring his battered psyche far more than the damn lotion he applied every single day to keep his skin supple.

Joe Shaughnessy glanced through dark-framed glasses perched on his hawkish nose, still-muscled shoulders bulging underneath plaid flannel. Like Ma, there was no sympathy in his eyes, ever. Or in his voice. At least, not now. But his brothers had told Patrick how, when Pop heard, he'd gone out into the postage stamp of a yard behind the house and bawled like a baby.

And for damn sure he'd hang them all by their gonads if he knew they'd ratted on him.

Already seated on the booster seat that had been a permanent fixture for years, Lilianna slurped her soup, dimpled fingers curled around her spoon. For her grandmother, she'd eat vegetable soup. For him, no way.

Patrick released a tense breath, then plopped beside her at the scarred wood table that had seen many an elbow fight over the years. Sunlight flooded the spotless room, gilding maple cabinets scrubbed so many times the original finish was but a memory, flashing off the same dented, decaled canister set that'd been there forever. Even the minimal updates they'd done ten or so years before—changing out the laminate counters, the cracked linoleum floors—had somehow left the comfortable shabbiness undisturbed.

Patrick pulled April's card from his shirt pocket, handed it to his father. "Got a lead on a job."

"Yeah?" Joe telescoped the card until it came into focus. Time for new glasses, apparently. "Where?"

"The old Rinehart place."

His father's eyes cut to his. "Somebody bought it?"

"One of her granddaughters decided to turn it back into an inn. Sam hooked us up."

His forehead knotted, Pop returned the card, broke off a piece of homemade bread and sopped up the broth left in the bottom of his bowl. "Last I heard, Amelia Rinehart had let the place go to rack and ruin. I'm surprised the girls didn't just unload it—"

"We had our wedding reception there, you know," his mother put in, setting a bowl of soup and two thick slices of bread in front of Patrick, then sitting at right angles to him. "Back in its heyday."

"Not to mention ours," Pop added with a chuckle.

Patrick frowned. "You did?"

Ma swatted at him with a crumpled napkin. "Go look at the wedding pictures on your way out, that's the Rinehart. Or was. It'd been in Amelia's husband's family for years, they turned it into an inn right after the war. Was quite the destination in these parts for some time. But after he died, she stopped taking in guests. Except for her three grand-daughters, every summer—"

"May I be s'cused?"

Ma leaned over to wipe Lili's soup-smeared face, then shooed her off. Only after they heard the clatter of toys being dumped out of the plastic bin in the living room did his mother say, "Old gal was a strange bird, no other way to put it. Rumor had it she rarely talked to her three daughters, even the one who stayed here in St. Mary's. But she loved her granddaughters. In her own way, at least." She leaned back, the space between her graying brows creased. More toys crashed. "You went to school with one of them, didn't you?"

"Melanie, yeah," Patrick said, spooning in a bite that was more potatoes and carrots than broth. "For a while. But she and her mother moved away before she graduated."

"That's right, they did—"

"You really think the gal's serious?" his father wedged in, clearly done with the small talk.

"Why wouldn't she be?"

"Because she'll probably go bankrupt in the process?"

"I'm guessing that's not an issue," Patrick said, which got a brow lift from his father. "She more or less indicated that money's no object. In any case, you got some time later this week?"

"Me? What do you need me for?"

Patrick had learned a lot since coming on board almost a year before, but he was still a rookie. And it was his dad's business. "It's looking to be a big job. I can design it, sure, but you're the expert at discussing time frames and giving estimates. Besides, people trust you—"

"That's a load of bull and you know it."

"About people trusting you?"

His father gave him a hard look. "No."

"Only trying to keep you in the loop," Patrick said, focusing again on his lunch.

"That's what cell phones are for—"

"I remember those girls as all being such pretty little things," his mother said, rising to clear Lilianna's bowl and cup. "The one who's sticking around—she grow up okay?"

"For God's sake, Kate," his dad said with a heavy sigh.

"What? I'm just making conversation, honestly! And you're the one pushing the boy to handle this on his own!"

Shoveling in another bite, Patrick let them bicker. Really, God love them for encouraging him to put himself back out there, to find a girl smart enough to appreciate him for who he was, for their refusal to accept his appearance as an impediment to that goal. Too bad he had no intention of following their well-intentioned advice. He'd taken enough risks—and suffered the consequences— for a lifetime, thank you. But it wasn't until he'd stopped fighting so hard to prove to himself, and everyone else, that nothing had changed that he'd finally learned to accept that everything had.

And with that acceptance came a kind of peace, one

that had barely begun to release him from the guilt and the self-pity, the nightmares he'd thought would choke him for the rest of his life. That first morning he'd awakened and realized he'd slept through the night he'd wept with gratitude. So for damn sure he'd hang on to that peace with everything he had in him. Not only for his sake, but for his daughter's, who deserved at least one coping parent.

One with both feet firmly planted in what *was,* not what *should have been.*

Or might be—

Patrick's cell rang. He dug it out of his shirt pocket, only to frown at the unfamiliar number before bringing the phone to his ear. "Patrick Shaughnessy—"

"Mr. Shaughnessy, it's April Ross."

His stomach jumped; there was more Southern in her voice than he remembered, something sweet and smoky that tried its damnedest to get inside him.

And letting his parents listen in to the conversation was not happening. He pushed away from the table to stalk out of the kitchen and down the hall.

"Ms. Ross. What can I do for you?"

"Would tomorrow morning work for you to come out? It occurred to me, what with it already being the end of October, we should probably get going as soon as possible. Don't you agree?"

This said as though her bolting like a scared rabbit had never happened. Interesting.

"Tomorrow would be fine. Around nine?"

"Perfect. We'll see you then."

We.

Replacing his phone, Patrick continued into his parents' jam-packed living room where Lili sat in front of the brick fireplace, holding a one-sided conversation with a bevy of beat-up dolls. At his entrance, she grinned up at him, and, as usual, his heart swelled. God, he loved this kid.

For her sake, he'd forced himself to smile again. To laugh. To appreciate the good in life and not give the bad the time of day. Trying to set a good example, like his parents had done for him. He squatted beside her, cupped her head. "Gotta go, munchkin. Give me a hug?" She scrambled to her feet and threw her arms around his neck. "You be good for Grandma, okay?"

He saw the flash of sadness in her dark eyes when she pulled away, but she only nodded and said, "'Kay."

Patrick called his goodbyes to his folks, then let himself out the front door, where the cold wind wreaked havoc with his face grafts, even for the short sprint to his truck. Sure, the idea of being around April Ross produced a kick to the gut the likes of which Patrick hadn't experienced in a long, long time. But after the hell he'd been through? A little lust was the least of his worries. Especially since this was a nonstarter. What with her being married and all.

And thank God for that.

Chapter Two

"That's not what you had on five minutes ago."

Shooting daggers at her cousin Melanie, April selected a coffee from the carousel on the gleaming, brand-new quartz counter and plopped it into the Keurig maker. The old kitchen, although huge, had been so outdated it nearly qualified for historical preservation status. And not in a good way. Now it was a chef's dream, with miles of countertops and cabinets, double ovens and a massive, stainless-steel-topped island, and—the *pièce de résis- tance*—a six-burner commercial-grade stove…in pink. Just for Mel. Who, now that true love had brought her back to St. Mary's after more than ten years away, had agreed— after much haranguing on April's part—to bring her mad cooking skills to the inn.

"I was cold," April said. "So I put on a heavier sweater."

"And changed your pants. And your headband—"

"Shut. Up."

"And that's your fourth cup of coffee this morning." The brunette grinned, her own mug of coffee nestled against her generous bosom, not so generously covered by a hot pink velour hoodie. Underneath long bangs, her gray-green eyes glittered. "That much caffeine and you're gonna sound like a chipmunk on speed. Although I do like that shade of purple on you."

Their other cousin, Blythe, an interior designer in D.C. who was there for a few days to check on the remodel's progress, wandered into the kitchen, yawning, a study in drapey grays and silvers. Tall, blond and impossibly chic, she frowned at April.

"Weren't you wearing something different at breakfast?"

Melanie poked Blythe as she bit into one of her own homemade cinnamon rolls. "I remember Patrick Shaughnessy. If vaguely. Dude's definitely worth the wardrobe crazies."

Her coffee brewed, April grabbed the porcelain mug, watching the sunlight dance across her rings before she turned and caught sight of the clock, a big, old-fashioned schoolroom thing Blythe had found in some antiques store. *Ten minutes.* Sighing, she leaned against the counter and looked at Mel. Time to reveal a detail or two she'd left out when she'd told them he was coming to give the estimate.

"I take it he was pretty good-looking back then?" she asked her cousin.

"In a craggy, Heathcliffian sort of way, yeah. All the Shaughnessy boys were."

"So his face…it wasn't scarred?"

"Scarred? You mean, like…a cut that didn't heal properly?"

"No. Worse. Like…I don't know. Burned, maybe?"

"What? Ohmigod, are you serious? Is it…bad?"

April nodded. "Although it's only one side of his face, so I didn't notice at first. But when I did…" She grimaced. "I sort of…freaked out."

Mel frowned. "Freaked out, how?"

"I ran. Like some frightened little twit who thought she'd seen the bogeyman. And yes, he saw the whole thing."

"Ouch," Blythe said.

"Exactly." April's gaze drifted out the new kitchen window, widened to take advantage of the shoreline view at the back of the property, the private dock jutting out into the glittering water. Her dock now. Her property. For a moment the thought made her feel all sparkly inside, until the guilt blotted it out again. "He has the sweetest little girl.…"

Out of the corner of her eye, she saw Blythe and Mel exchange a glance. Deciding to ignore it, April faced them again. "I actually went back to apologize, but he'd already left. So that's my first order of business when he gets here."

Blythe's eyebrows dipped. "To apologize? You sure that's a good idea?"

"You got a better one?"

"Yeah. Act like it never happened."

"Oh, right—"

"I'm serious," the blonde said, her short, spiked hair like frosted glass in the sunshine. "Look, I get you feel like crap, but he's probably used to it—"

"So that makes what I did okay?"

"No. But the last thing you want to do is make him more uncomfortable, right?"

Conflicted, April looked to Mel. "So what would you do?"

"Me? I would've hired another landscaper. Maybe. Hey," Mel said when April rolled her eyes, "all you can do is trust your gut. Do what feels right."

The doorbell rang. Straightening, she set her mug on

the counter and swiped her suddenly damp palms down the front of her jeans. "If I don't throw up first," she muttered, then headed toward the door, which, after a lung-searing breath, she opened.

Only to run smack into that crystalline gaze, boring directly into hers.

He'd never in his life seen someone blush that hard. April kept swallowing, too, like she was about to be sick. Patrick took pity on her and held up his clipboard, to remind her of his purpose there. Except she shook her head, making her red-gold hair swish softly over her shoulders and Patrick unaccountably irritated. Although about what, he couldn't have said.

What he could say, though, was that she was even prettier than he remembered. As in, short-out-the-brain pretty. If a trifle too put together for his taste, what with her sweater, shoes and headband all matching. She was also obviously broken up about what she'd done, even before she said, "Before we get started…there is no excuse for how I acted the other day. And I'm sorry."

Frankly, he was torn, between wanting to let her off the hook and wanting to see her squirm. His face took some getting used to, no two ways around it. So taking offense was pointless. People were just people.

But something about this one especially provoked him. Maybe because he wasn't entirely buying the whole innocent act she was trying so hard to sell.

Patrick slid his hands into his back pockets, narrowing his eyes even as he realized she'd kept hers steady on his face. Like she was trying to prove something, probably more to herself than to him.

"How you acted?"

She swallowed again. And somehow turned even redder. Had to give her props, though, for not sending out her husband in her stead. Then again, for all he knew this was one of those projects where the wife handled all the design decisions and the man just signed the checks. They got a lot of those. "Yes," she finally said. "At the garden center."

"Can't say as I noticed anything."

"And now you're messing with me."

His brows crashed together. What was left of them, anyway. "I'm not—"

"The heck you aren't. Because you know darn well what I'm talking about. Although if it makes you feel better, let me spell it out. I acted like a total dimwit when I noticed your scars. I don't know why, I certainly wasn't raised like that, and there's no way I could live with myself without apologizing for my bad behavior. And no, you're under no obligation to accept my apology, but I am obligated to give it. So. You ready to get started or what?"

For a good five, six seconds, Patrick could only gape at April like, as she put it, a total dimwit. Sure, her wanting to make amends probably stemmed more from ingrained good manners than anything else, but there'd been a fire behind her words that gave him pause. That, and that damned steady gaze, which was rattling him to hell and back.

"Apology accepted," he heard himself mutter, then cleared his throat. "You might want to put on a coat or something, it's pretty cold out here."

She nodded, then vanished into the house, only to return a minute or so later with another woman, a tall blonde who looked vaguely familiar.

"This is my cousin, Blythe Broussard," April said, wrapped up in an expensive-looking tan coat that fell well below her knees. "She's overseeing the house remodel, but she's also got some ideas for the landscaping."

Still no husband. Interesting.

And maybe the guy simply isn't here at the moment—

And this was nuts. He'd worked with plenty of female clients before, but this was the first time he could remember giving even half a thought to who they lived with, or were married to, or whatever. Mentally slapping himself, Patrick turned his attention to Blythe, who also met his gaze dead-on. Although, unlike her cousin, she'd probably been forewarned.

"Then let's get started," he said, waving the clipboard toward the gouged, muddy front yard—a fitting symbol for his life if ever there was one. "After you, ladies."

She'd let Blythe do most of the talking that day. For many reasons, not the least of which was that Blythe had a far better handle on matters horticultural than April did. Or probably ever would. But for another, even though she'd gotten the apology out fine, the way Patrick had looked at her afterward had practically rendered her mute.

Although whether the condition was temporary or not remained to be seen, she thought as she pulled up outside the generic warehouse building on the other side of town, the unpaved parking lot littered with assorted trucks ranging in size from massive to gargantuan, not to mention all manner of digging and hauling equipment.

It'd been a week since the appointment. She'd assumed Patrick would send or drop off the plans and estimate at the inn, but the secretary who'd called had said he'd prefer she come to the office for the presentation. So here she was, clutching closed her Harris Tweed blazer as she trooped through the wind toward the door. At Clay's urging, she'd gradually ditched her old wardrobe in favor of the classier—and more classic—items he'd kindly suggested would better reflect her new status. Hence the blazer. And the designer riding boots. But since moving back to St. Mary's, she'd also reacquainted herself with jeans and the loose, comfy sweaters she'd once loved, even if she no longer had to rely on thrift stores or seventy-five-percent-off sales to buy them.

Instead of the middle-aged woman she'd heard on the phone, an older man in black-rimmed glasses sat behind the battered desk, his navy hoodie zipped up underneath a canvas coat as work worn as the desk. But his grin, set in a clefted chin, eased the nervousness she'd refused to fully acknowledge until that moment.

"Ms. Ross, right?" he said, rising and extending a rough hand.

"Yes—"

"I'm Joe, Patrick's dad. He's on the horn, but go on back to the conference room. We don't stand on ceremony around here. You want some coffee?" He pointed to the standard-issue Mr. Coffee on the metal cart in front of the paneled wall. "It's fresh, Marion made it before she ran to the bank—"

"Oh…no, thanks, I'm good."

"Okay, then. It's straight back, you can't miss it."

She heard Patrick before she saw him, his rich, deep laughter making her breath catch. That he *could* laugh like that made blood rush to her cheeks all over again. The conference "room" was nothing more than a collection of tables and folding chairs, no interior walls, with a big-screen TV—which probably cost more than the rest of the furniture altogether—mounted on the paneling on the far side of the space.

His cell phone clamped to his ear, Patrick lounged in the far chair with one work-booted foot propped on the table in front of him, his "good" side to her. Focused on his conversation, he didn't see her at first. It was a nice

face, April decided, although Mel was right—you couldn't
call it exactly handsome. Honest, though. Good lines. A
man's face, she decided, one befitting someone older than
his late twenties, since she guessed he was about the same
age as Mel. Which made him a year or so older than her—

She suddenly realized he'd noticed her, his expression
downgrading to neutral as he lowered his foot, then stood,
pocketing his phone.

"Sorry. Didn't see you standing there."

Her stomach fluttered, from nerves, from something
much worse, as she smiled. "It's okay. I didn't want to in-
terrupt you."

He nodded, then waved her in. "Have a seat, then. This
won't take too long."

The coolness in his voice made April cringe. For all
his assurance the other day that he'd accepted her apology, there was no mistaking the change in his demeanor
once he'd noticed her presence. Not that she expected everyone in the world to like her, but it killed her to think
she'd done something, unwittingly or not, to hurt another
human being.

Then again, she thought as she sat on one of the metal
chairs, she'd been as sincere as she knew how when she'd
tried to undo her gaffe. True, she couldn't imagine what
he'd been through, but despite this annoying quirk that
made her want to resolve every problem life tossed in her
path, she had to remind herself it wasn't any of her business. Goodness, even Clayton had tried his best to convince her that, oddly enough, the entire world was not her
responsibility. Breaking the habits of a lifetime, though—
not so easy.

And keeping this relationship strictly professional would
be one small, important step toward that goal. Contractor
and client—this, she could do.

Then an image of what she realized could be the inn's front yard appeared on the screen—a yard filled with stone paths and flower beds, blooming fruit trees and lush bushes. Of seating areas nestled into several outdoor "rooms." A pair of evergreens flanking the porch steps, a hedge of roses alongside a low stone wall. And more, much more than she could take in.

"It could really look like that?"

"It really could," Patrick said from several feet away, then began to explain what she was looking at, periodically adjusting the image as he took her on a virtual tour, his obvious enthusiasm for his work leaching past April's not-so-hot-to-begin-with defenses. "The idea is to make it an all-season landscape—hence the evergreens. To decorate for the holidays, if you like."

In the heat of the moment, their gazes met. Tangled. April quickly returned her attention to the screen. Not making that mistake again, nope.

"Oh...yes," she said, willing her heart to stop pounding. "Perfect."

"And in the back..." He clicked a few keys, and the backyard appeared. "A gazebo for weddings. Or whatever."

Her throat clogged. "It's absolutely amazing."

"It also doesn't come cheap."

Ah, yes. Money. Business. *Stay on track.* "I wouldn't imagine that it does."

"Figured I may as well give you the full monty, we can always cut back if we have to." He reached for a slim folder beside the computer, handed it to her. "Here's the estimate, with a complete breakdown for materials and labor. See what you think."

April pulled out the papers, scanned them, flipped to the last page, had a brief pang of conscience—considering all those years when she couldn't even buy her mother flowers—then held out her hand. "Got a pen?"

Clearly, Patrick hadn't expected that. "You sure? I mean, no questions—?"

"Nope." She dug her checkbook out of her purse, discovered a pen already in it. "Never mind, I have a pen. I take it you'd like half down now?"

"Actually, we do it in thirds—"

She wrote out the amount, signed the contract, then handed it back to him with the check. "So when can you start?"

He separated the copies from the original, slipped hers into another folder, then set the folder in front of her. "Next week? The weather looks like it's going to stay decent at least through the middle of the month."

"Great," she said, getting to her feet, then extending her hand, which he took. Another mistake, but too late now. And the sizzling would subside eventually.

The folder tucked against her side, she started out the door, wanting to get away from that intense, puzzled gaze. But he stopped her with, "I don't get it."

She turned, frowning. "Pardon?"

"Why you didn't haggle."

"Was I supposed to?"

"People…usually do."

Somehow, she caught the subtext. "Rich people, you mean?"

She thought his cheeks might've colored. "Didn't say that."

"But that's what you meant."

"Okay. Yeah." His crossed his arms, high on his chest. "In my experience the better off the client, the more they're inclined to try to get a better deal. But you didn't. Why?"

By rights, his borderline impudence—not to mention his

assumption that all rich people thought and acted the same way—should have ticked her off. And probably would have, except for the genuine mystification underpinning his words. As well as her having to admit there'd been a time not that long ago when she might've been tempted to do some pigeonholing of her own. So she didn't take particular offense. Nor, in theory, was she under any obligation to explain herself.

Except this little exchange had only illustrated what she'd already learned, which was that people treated you differently when they thought you had money. And not always in a good way. So if she was going to be judged, at least let it be on who she was, not on who Patrick thought she was.

Maybe it wasn't up to her to right all the wrongs in the world, but she could at least address this one.

His mother had always said his big mouth was going to get him in trouble one day. Judging from the look on April's face, Patrick figured that day had come. But she was like…like a little hoppy toad, never doing what he expected. Making him crazy.

"Sorry," he muttered. "That was out of line."

So of course she laughed. And, yes, he almost jumped.

"It's okay, I'm used to dealing with people who say whatever's on their mind. My mother-in-law was like that, and we got on like gangbusters. Then again, I get on with most human beings. I kind of see it like my mission in life. Anyway…" She waggled her left hand, the rings glinting in the overhead light, "the thing is, I didn't always have money. To be blunt…I married into it."

"Really. Another…mission?"

She laughed again, then glanced down at the rings, the light dimmed in her eyes when she looked up again. "No.

Not at all. But what I'm saying is, this is still pretty new for me. Believe me I know what it's like to try to make a living. To hopefully get an honest day's pay for an honest day's work, and then—" she sighed "—to wonder if that's going to be enough to meet the bills. So I can't tell you what a relief it is to not worry about money any more. To be able to sign that contract without a second thought."

Or any thought, apparently. "Did you even get other bids?"

"I considered it. Of course. But for one thing, your ratings on Angie's List are through the roof. And for another, based on your discussions with Blythe, she gave me a ball-park figure for what it would probably cost. And you were right on target." She pulled a face. "It also doesn't seem fair to make other companies go to all that trouble when only one can get the job."

"It's just business, Mrs. Ross."

"True. But sometimes you have to trust your instincts. This is one of those times." Then she chuckled. "Unless you deliberately padded the estimate?"

"No!" he said, only to smile himself when she chuckled again. "Although it will be nice to make a halfway decent profit margin on a job, for once. Especially since Christmas is coming. Bonuses for our workers," he said when she frowned. "They were pretty lame last year, although they all said they understood. At least we didn't have to lay off anyone, but it was touch-and-go there for a while—"

What the hell? Talking about the business, especially with a client…he never did that. Ever.

Her expression softening, she shouldered her giant purse and pulled on her gloves. Good leather, he was guessing. As were the boots. And the purse. Maybe she hadn't been born into wealth, but she wore it well all the same.

"Something tells me it's going to be real nice working with you all," she said, then looked around. Although God knew what she thought she was seeing. Then her gaze touched his again. "I know this is really pushing it, but…do you think it'll be done by Thanksgiving? I'd love to have my parents come stay. My mother hasn't been back to the house for nearly thirty years."

His phone rang. But since it wasn't his mother's ring, or his sister Frannie's, he ignored it, figuring it wasn't anything that couldn't wait five minutes. "The planting will have to be done in stages, some specimens don't take kindly to establishing over the winter. But all the brick-work, the walks and walls…those, we can do. I promise, we'll have it looking pretty good by then."

She grinned. "No more mud?"

"No more mud," Patrick said, nearly overcome, as he watched her walk away, with something that felt an awful lot like envy, that some other dude had it better than him. An indulgence he hadn't allowed since he woke up in the VA hospital. And one damned if he was going to allow now.

Then he remembered to check his voice mail, only to feel his gut turn inside out when he heard Natalie's voice, saying she wanted to see Lilianna that weekend, was it okay?

Okay? No. Since every time his ex blew into town and disrupted their daughter's routine, it took a solid week to get Lili back on track. Four-year-olds weren't good with change. Or understanding why Mama kept disappearing. But it wasn't like he could deny either of them some time together. And, if nothing else, dealing with that would take his mind off pretty, married, out-of-his-league clients.

Although he had a good idea it would take a lot more than his ex's shenanigans, or even his daughter's inevitable bad mood as a result, to expunge April Ross from his thoughts.

* * *

"Yes, you need to leave," Blythe had said. "And not return until I've finished your suite. Because you hover, that's why. And I've already called Aunt Tilda, told her you're coming. She's thrilled."

Hence, three days later, April found herself staring out of her parents' Richmond condo at the bleak November sky hanging over a dozen condos that looked exactly like this one. Not that she had any right to turn up her nose, since she'd helped them pick it out. Only she'd never planned on spending any real time here herself.

And, as her mother bustled about in the open kitchen behind her, listening to talk radio at full volume as she made lunch, she remembered why.

She loved her parents, don't get her wrong. Enough to freak out when her father became seriously ill, to worry when her mother had to quit her job to take care of him, enough to make sacrifices on their behalf she doubted few women her age would have dreamed of making. Even if, at the end, she'd didn't feel she'd sacrificed all that much. But she'd forgotten how stubborn her mother could be. A propensity inherited from Mama's own mother, most likely, since nobody could hold on to things—newspapers, margarine tubs, grudges—like Nana.

"It's a simple invitation," April said, swallowing down the irritation, the hurt. Fine, so maybe she'd led her mother to believe they were renovating Nana's house to sell it. Meaning, yes, she'd deliberately kept her parents in the dark about buying out her cousins, about her plans, because April was having enough trouble convincing herself she could make a go of this without throwing her mother's inevitable disapproval into the mix. So why she'd thought presenting it as a fait accompli would garner a better reaction, she had no idea. Because clearly it hadn't.

"And you know I can't set foot back in that house," Mama said behind her. "I just can't."

April turned away from the window, thinking that—from a distance, anyway—with her ash-blond pixie haircut and still-trim figure, her mother looked far younger than she was. "Except it's my house now—"

"It's still tainted, April. With all those bad memories…" Her mother shut her eyes, shaking her head. "So many bad memories."

Although how terrible her mother's memories really were, April wondered. Lord knew Nana had been irascible and strict, and from all accounts had given her three daughters far less freedom than most children of their generation—prompting all three girls to rebel by marrying men Nana heartily disapproved of. And which, in turn, led her grandmother to cut all three of them off. Warm and fuzzy, Nana had not been.

But while her grandmother might've been a pain in the butt, April had no reason to believe she'd ever been out-and-out abusive. And weirdly enough she hadn't let the rifts between her and her daughters tarnish her relationship with her granddaughters. Not when they were kids, at least. Those summers at the beach house with Blythe and Mel—summers when April could, for six or eight weeks, forget her own chaotic homelife—had been the high points of her childhood.

"I know you and Nana had your differences," April said gently, "but she and I didn't—"

"Why, April? *Why?*" Her mother squawked the last word like her neck was being wrung. "Even if the place weren't a money pit, which you know it is, for you to, to do this without telling us, to throw away everything Clayton left you…I don't understand, April. I really don't. You could have bought any house you liked—"

"Because I don't want *any* place, I want *this* one. I love the Rinehart, Mama," she said when her mother pursed her lips. "I always have. And now, unbelievably, it's all mine. *My* money pit." Although what she'd spent on the house so far had barely made a dent in the inheritance. Of course, she knew she couldn't coast on that forever, that if the inn didn't turn a profit within a reasonable time she wouldn't be able to keep it going. A worry for another day, however. "Besides, you wouldn't recognize it now, what with everything Blythe's done. And especially once the landscaping's complete."

Which, unfortunately, wouldn't be before April's return.

Too bad, that. Since, now that April had put some space between herself and Patrick Shaughnessy's lethal gaze and could look at things with something resembling objectivity, she had to admit two things: one, that she was seriously attracted to the man, which she supposed, given her…situation and the before mentioned lethal gaze, wasn't really a stretch; but that, two, the timing couldn't be worse for her to be attracted to anybody.

"No," her mother said again, shaking her head, and it took April a moment to click back into the conversation. "When your grandmother threw me out, I vowed I'd never return. And I don't renege on my promises."

Yeah, back to that stubbornness thing. As witness her mother's never giving up on April's father, no matter how many times he'd propose yet another "brilliant" get-rich scheme that inevitably fizzled out, but only after blowing through whatever savings they had. A good man, a kind man, but with the business acumen—and sense—of a gerbil.

So her mother going on about April's "throwing her money away" was just a trifle inconsistent. That said, at least her parents were still together. Yes, her mother's intractability about never going near Nana's house again was annoying as all get-out, but the woman sure knew how to stick to her guns…and stand by her man, no matter what. As she said, she didn't break her promises.

And neither did April.

Mama carted a plate of sandwiches to the dinette table on the other side of the counter, calling April's father before setting them down. "And what on earth put the idea in your head to be an innkeeper, anyway?"

"I suppose because I like taking care of people. Feeling useful."

Her mother dusted her hands, then crossed her arms, censure softening into concern. An unexpected shift that caught April off guard. "I would have thought you'd already done that. More than enough for one lifetime."

April's forehead scrunched. "What? Oh. You mean, because of Clay?"

"Exactly. Because…" Mama glanced toward the hall, then lowered her voice. "Because after taking care of your father all those months, I know how hard that must've been on you. At the…at the end."

"But this isn't even remotely the same thing—"

"And for you to lose your husband so early," her mother went on, clearly determined to keep this particular train off track, "it was so unfair, honey. Especially since…well."

Especially since she and Clayton hadn't had children. But then Mama wasn't privy to the particulars. Probably never would be, either, it being a nonissue now. Because if she had known…oh, Lord. Woman would've had a fit and fallen into it.

And for somebody who considered herself an honest person, April had more secrets than a TV preacher.

Mama cleared her throat. "What Clayton did for us… I still thank him in my prayers every day. Thank God that he was in our lives, even if only for such a short time. He truly was the most generous man on earth."

"Yes. He was—"

"Then, baby, don't you think, after what you've been through, he'd want you to take things easy? To enjoy life?"

Laughing, April went to the kitchen for a pitcher of tea. "I'm only twenty-six, Mama. Not sure how I'm supposed to enjoy life without living it. To…" She swung the tea pitcher, making her mother suck in a breath. "Embrace unexpected opportunities."

Her mother hurried over to rescue the hapless pitcher, clutching it to her stomach as she stared at April. "By running an inn?"

"By realizing my dream, of having my own business, doing what I love to do. *That's* what Clayton would have wanted for me. And that's the best way I know how to honor him," she added before her mother could shoehorn in another protest. Which she did, anyway.

"But it doesn't make sense—"

Mama clamped shut her mouth as Daddy finally shuffled in from their bedroom where he'd been watching TV, grunting appreciatively at the array of sandwiches before lowering himself into his chair with a contented sigh. Although thinner than he used to be, Edward Ross was otherwise remarkably fit for someone who'd all but rubbed shoulders with death not three years before, even if his entrepreneurial days were in all likelihood behind him. And praise Jesus for that. But what brought tears to April's eyes was knowing that, thanks to Clayton, her parents' needs would be met for the rest of their lives. That in exchange for putting her dreams on hold for a few years, he'd now given her the freedom to follow them.

Wherever they led her.

And however scary they were.

A thrill of anticipation shunted through her as she turned to her mother and said softly, "And you of all people should understand that what makes us happy isn't necessarily what makes sense."

Another moment or two passed before her mother muttered, "Then you're as much of a blamed fool as the rest of us," before carting the pitcher over to the table to pour her husband his tea. Only as April opened her mouth to refute her mother's statement, she couldn't seem to shove the words past a certain somebody's lethal blue gaze.

Lethal...and, unless she was sadly mistaken, needy.

Yeah. What Mama said.

Chapter Three

Patrick saw Lilianna's face crumple and thought, *It's too damn early for this*. And the thing was, the morning had gone reasonably well so far. She hadn't given him grief over what he'd picked for her to wear—blue tights, green tutu, the first hoodie he put his hands on. Or the scrambled egg and OJ he'd plunked down in front of her while she watched Sesame Street from his sister's cast-off bistro table in the funky little apartment on the top floor of an equally funky little carriage house in town, not far from his parents. Except then she'd asked for a Toaster Strudel and it all went south.

Because, in his hurry to get the kid fed and over to his mother's before his crew started wondering where the hell he was, he accidentally let a ribbon of frosting dribble onto the plastic Tinkerbelle plate.

"Baby, baby…it's okay," Patrick said over the resulting wail. "Just scoop it up with your finger and suck it off, no biggee."

"I c-can't." Tiny arms clamped over little chest. "You *r-rooned* it."

Patrick sighed, knowing the dramatics had far less to do with his sloppy frosting technique than it did Natalie's in-and-out visit the day before. For hours after his ex's departure, Lili had clung to him like a little monkey, thumb in mouth, bursting into inconsolable tears when he finally had to put her down to visit the john. To be fair, he knew Nat felt bad about the arrangement, but the support system and Patrick's job were here in St. Mary's, and Nat's school was in Philly, and they'd both agreed Lili needed the stability more than she needed her yet-to-get-her-act-together mother. But how did you explain that to a little kid?

However, even though he hated seeing Lili so miserable, his own mother would smack him into next week for indulging the tantrum. So he squatted beside her at the table and said softly, "Eat it or not, makes no difference to me. But sometimes things don't turn out the way we want them to." He cupped her curly head, leaned over to kiss her puckered brow before standing again, crossing to the coffeemaker to fill his thermos. Giving her some space. "All you can do is deal with it."

Although whether any of that made any sense or not to a four-year-old, God only knew. Especially since he was still feeling his way with this *daddy* thing. Heck, he barely saw her until she was three, and even then he wasn't around all that much, since his life at that point still revolved around seemingly endless, and often excruciating, therapies and treatments. And when he was with her, he was constantly battling both frustration and guilt that he couldn't be the kind of hands-on parent he'd envisioned.

Not to mention husband.

Patrick skimmed a hand over his close-cropped hair—since the burns had eaten half his scalp, there was no point trying to grow out the hair on the side that still functioned properly. No wonder Natalie left him. Not what she'd signed up for, either. Yeah, you could go on about how nobody gets to choose what life throws in their path, but the fact remained that some people handled the crap better than others. That was life, too. So while, sure, it'd hurt that Nat hadn't been able to cope, neither had he been surprised—

"All done."

Thermos in hand, Patrick turned to see his grinning daughter holding up her empty plate, pink cheeks smeared with blueberry filling and frosting, and his heart melted more than the frosting. Then he chuckled.

"Guess you were hungry, huh?"

"Yep," Lili said, giggling, all signs of Cranky Baby vanished. Patrick grabbed a wet paper towel to clean her up, plunked her dish in the dishwasher, then hauled her out of the chair to let her do the baby monkey thing, more determined than ever that nobody was gonna hurt his little girl.

Ever.

Despite his best efforts, Patrick still arrived at the job site after his crew. Good thing, then, he'd reviewed the plans with them well enough that they'd already begun prepping the site, yanking out dead trees and bushes, grading the lot in order to lay the walkways and driveway Blythe and he had codesigned.

Speaking of whom…in jeans and some baggy, drapey thing that made her look like a large blond moth, April's cousin traipsed across the muddy yard, reaching his truck as he got out.

"Sorry I'm late," he muttered, grabbing his thermos from the cup holder before slamming shut the door.

"Not a problem, your guys seem to have everything under control."

Patrick grunted, then said, "April around?"

"No, she's at her folks for a few days, she'll be back later in the week."

He'd been right that Natalie's visit, and the resulting fallout, had more or less shoved thoughts about April Ross to the back of his brain. Except the minute he got back in his truck after dropping Lili off at his mom's, it was like the floodgates opened. The whole way out here, in fact, all he could think about *was* April. In ways he had no right to think about a married woman. It'd been years since he'd been to confession—figuring, he supposed, that since he'd already been through hell, God would cut him some slack—but even Patrick had to admit he'd probably have some serious atoning to do with this one.

So it'd been with a mix of trepidation and anticipation that he'd pulled up to her house, expecting to see her. Hear her voice. See her smile. That light in her eyes that seared straight through him. Gave him, for lack of a better word, hope.

Only she wasn't here. And for some reason his brain was having a real hard time processing that information.

Which might account for why he then said to Blythe, "Her husband go with her?"

The blonde frowned. "Her husband?"

"Yeah. Not that I've ever seen him, but…" He pointed to his own left hand, the base of his ring finger still slightly indented. "Her rings?"

"Oooh." Blythe pressed her lips together, like she wasn't sure what to say next. "I forget not everyone knows. April's husband passed away, Patrick. Several months before she returned to St. Mary's."

"What?"

Blythe smiled. Gently. "Yep, she's a widow."

And if he'd thought he was having trouble processing things before… "But she's still wearing her rings."

"Yeah. She is." Blythe briefly squeezed his shoulder, then walked away, and Patrick's brain finally kicked in enough to remind him if there was one thing worse than fantasizing about a married woman, it was fantasizing about one still mourning her dead husband.

There weren't enough Hail Marys in the world.

Later that week—after Blythe had given her the all clear—a small but potent thrill shimmied through April as she pulled onto the road that led back to St. Mary's Cove.

Back *home.*

Wow. What a concept. She'd never fully realized how much she'd always thought of the tiny town in that way, even as a kid. Especially as a kid, when visiting her grandmother's house each summer had been the only constant in a life that was always starting over.

And now she never had to leave again, April thought as the Lexus purred down Main Street, past quaint shops and quirky cafés, mom-and-pop businesses that somehow kept chugging along despite recessions and suburban sprawl. Unless she wanted to, that is. And, boy, was she done with starting over. As exciting as watching the house's resurrection had been, she couldn't wait for it to be finished so she could get on with living. Instead of…waiting. As if her life thus far had been a series of canal locks, and she'd finally passed through the last one before the open sea.

Several minutes later, she squinted as the house came into view, glowing peach in the setting sun, and she spotted one of the Shaughnessy and Sons trucks parked off to the side, like a hulking black bear having a snooze. And, yep, her insides flinched. In that "Oh, goody," but not, kind of way.

Sigh.

Because although April had nothing against family traditions per se, some of them—like, say, being a blamed fool—really shouldn't be upheld. Logic kept neatly laying out all the reasons why fantasizing about a certain dangerous-looking landscaper was the bad idea to end all bad ideas. Yet this screechy little voice kept whispering: *Screw logic* and *Go for it* and *What have you got to lose?*

Heh. Good one.

Batting away the whisperings like gnats on a summer's night, April climbed out of the car…and her mouth fell open. Was that the same yard she'd left less than a week before?

A new driveway snaked around what clearly would be a formal garden, complete with some sort of sculpture/fountain in the center that was elegant and whimsical and cutting edge, all at once. Lots of angles, lots of curves. Copper, maybe? Thin, graceful evergreens flanked the porch, giving way to all kinds of bushes and things she couldn't even begin to identify. It wasn't entirely finished, of course—she could see large patches of dirt where she assumed more plantings would go, the beginnings of several stone pathways winding through the flower beds—but what was there was spectacular.

"So what do you think?"

Patrick's low voice behind her nearly made her piddle her pants. She turned, wondering what it was about the half light that turned dangerous into downright delicious. She didn't even see the scars anymore—well, she *saw* them, sure, but she also saw past them. More to the point, she *felt* him. His presence or aura or whatever the heck he exuded, like a bonfire threatening to consume her.

This was beyond bad, wasn't it?

"I love it," she finally got out, fingering her rings as she ripped her gaze from his mouth. "Y'all got a lot accomplished in such a short time."

"There's bad weather forecast for the weekend. I was trying to beat it."

Hmm. Sounded friendly enough, but—she glanced back—no smile, no light in the eyes, nothing. Was it her, or was she the only one here being attacked by the lust demons? Nasty wee beasties. Then again, given the hard time she was having catching a breath, maybe not so wee—

"Daddy? Where are you?"

"Out front, baby."

A moment later, little footsteps pounded on the porch, down the steps, curls bouncing as a visual cacophony of stripes and florals and a half-dozen colors catapulted into her father's arms, sending the demons scattering to the four winds.

Although the fire…not so much. True, the warmth shifted north to spread through April's chest, to the base of her throat. But the ache of seeing him hold his little girl consumed her every bit as much as what, moments before, had produced some very imprudent thoughts. Then Patrick gave April a look over his daughter's head, not of fear, exactly, but certainly wariness.

Don't take it as a challenge, don't—

Mel rushed outside, hair a fright, hoodie unzipped, jeans hugging curves April could only dream of, whooshing out a breath when she saw Lilianna in her father's arms.

"You little scamp," her cousin mildly scolded over the little girl's giggles, and April thought, *Huh?* "You got away from me! Man, I'd forgotten how slippery little kids can be! April!" A grin spread across Mel's face. "You're back! Good! Dinner's almost ready—"

"We'd better be going, then," Patrick said as a few more *Huhs?* pinged around in April's brain.

"The heck you will, I've made enough food for half the town. No arguments. Besides, I'm sure Lili wants to taste the cake she helped bake. Wouldn't you, sweetie?"

Cue vigorous head shake. Big eyes and soft "Uh-huh." April melting into puddle of goo. Granted, children had been known to get the goo flowing for some time already, but this one...

"Now how could you possibly say no to that?" Mel asked Patrick, and April thought, *How, indeed?* And, indeed, the big, buff man holding the itty-bitty girl in his big, buff arms made light of things and said in that case, of course they'd stay. But with definite *only because it's not worth the fight* undertones.

Undertones which her cousin either didn't pick up or chose to ignore. April was betting on the latter. "I've been experimenting," Mel said. "Still getting used to the stove. Ryder should be here momentarily—" And yes, at the mention of her fiancé, her cousin went a bit gooey herself. "He's fetching Quinn from her piano lesson. Well, just don't stand there. Come on in."

So everyone trooped through the enlarged entryway leading into the new-and-holy-cow-improved gathering room. "Blythe said she was sorry she couldn't be here," Mel went on, oblivious to Patrick's decided lack of enthusiasm, "she had some kind of 'emergency' appointment back in D.C. But she said to let her know if she needs to change anything in your suite." Then she grinned at Lilianna. "Hey, cutie-patootie, wanna come help set the table?"

"Yeah, sure," the little girl said, then wriggled out of her daddy's arms to bounce off after Mel, while Patrick watched her as though worried she'd vanish through a magic portal into an alternate universe. And wasn't that cute as all get-out? Although, when puberty came calling? She wasn't sure who to pity more, Lili or Patrick.

Looking away, April felt the house's warm glow curl around her, the smells from the kitchen bringing tears to her eyes. A lot had gone on inside, as well, during her absence. Serious miracle worker, that Blythe. April couldn't wait to get photos up on the Rinehart's new website, although too bad there wasn't a way to let potential guests experience the aromas, as well. Tears threatened again. If it hadn't been for Clayton…

"You okay?"

Not alone. Right. April nodded, clearing her throat, trying to ignore the beasties tiptoeing back. Beasties too dense to realize *the man didn't want to be here.*

"If you'd told me four years ago," she said, not looking at him, "that I'd be getting ready to open my own business, that this place would be mine…" She turned, taking in the refinished floors, the warm colors and inviting overstuffed furniture, the framed watercolors Blythe had bought from a local artist. Sigh. "We really can't predict what life has in store for us, can we?"

Long pause. "We sure as hell can't."

Oh, Lord. Speaking of dense. "I'm so sorry, I didn't mean—"

"I know you didn't. It's okay."

She hazarded a glance. Met his gaze. Blushed in places she didn't normally blush, a sensation simultaneously pleasant and unsettling. "You also don't *have* to stay."

Patrick shoved his hands in his pockets, clearly not realizing what that did to the front of his jeans. "There's a kid in your kitchen who might beg to differ. Not to mention your cousin." Another pause. "And whatever your cousin's making is bound to be better than packaged mac and cheese."

Wow. Were they having an actual conversation? "That's really pathetic."

"It's one of a handful of things Lili will eat."

"And the others are?"

"Toaster Strudel, broccoli, sometimes an egg. And my mother's vegetable soup."

April laughed, confusing the heck out of the beasties. Not to mention herself. "You have a very strange child."

"Tell me something I don't know," he said. Deadpan. Which was not making him *less* sexy. "By the way," he added, "I haven't been bringing her every day. But both my mom and my sister are dealing with some kind of bug. Your cousin was here and she kind of…" He frowned. "Took over."

"That's Mel. Not that I wouldn't have done the same thing." She shrugged. "Lili's a sweetheart. You're welcome to bring her any time you want."

He nodded, muttering, "Thanks," almost as an after-thought.

April cleared her throat. "So…Lili's mother…?"

"We're divorced."

And, oh, there were questions she was dying to ask. Like how young *were* they when they got married, why he appeared to have full custody of his daughter, if Lili even ever saw her mom, that sort of thing.

The very sort of thing smart cookies knew to tiptoe right past.

Patrick tried to act normal during dinner, at least for Lilianna's sake, even though it was bugging the life out of him that he hadn't taken advantage of April's not-so-subtle prying to ask *her* about her husband. You know, give her the chance to come clean?

But he hadn't, and she hadn't, so best simply to let the

whole thing drop, right? After all, what did it matter in the big, or even small, scheme of things?

Still, he could not wait to get out of here. To take his child and book it back to their little apartment, where things were safe and predictable and he couldn't hear April's laughter. Or see those blasted rings sparkling in the candlelight.

Ever since discovering April was a widow, Patrick had redoubled his efforts to give his untoward musings the boot. A task that should not have been the bear it seemed determined to be, given that he was hardly a stranger to disciplining his thoughts. Otherwise he'd probably be dead by now. And, fool that he was, he'd actually thought he'd succeeded, keeping his focus on Lili, on the job, on working out, on Lili, so there was no room for anything else.

Until there April was, again, and now he understood the shadows in her eyes, which weren't making things better. See, realizing he had to love Lili enough for two parents—before he was even sure he knew how to love her enough for one—had been a kick in the butt to his basic humanity, too. That he couldn't love Lili, not the way she deserved to be loved, without having empathy for his other fellow beings.

No matter how much he'd wanted to shut himself off.

"Okay, cake!" Mel said, duck-walking with outstretched arms behind Lili as the little girl carried in the three-tier concoction, her pleased grin nearly splitting her face in two, and April's gaze snagged Patrick's just long enough for him to catch something *else* in her eyes.

Not to mention the blush sweeping up her neck.

Well, hell. How had he missed that?

It may have been a while, but unless he was mistaken the gal had the hots for him. Embarrassed as all hell about it, too, was his guess. Which he should have found gratifying, if not flattering. Or at least highly amusing. Since she was obviously channeling her grief in…other directions, there was no way in hell he was letting either of them go there.

Because he'd amassed enough regrets for one lifetime already. And she'd get over it. Especially once the inn opened and—he took a bite of the cake, which he had to admit was crazy good, even if he wasn't a huge chocolate fan—word got out about her cousin's cooking. Yep, April was going to be far too busy to think about…whatever she was thinking about.

Even so, much later, after he and Lili had returned home and he'd read *Go, Dog. Go!* three times before she finally conked out, after the unseasonably warm night had enticed him out onto the staircase clinging to the side on the brick building, he felt the darkness that had never completely left inside him stir, and stretch, and shift into something that felt an awful lot like yearning.

Which would never do.

April's mother had always been big on that whole "see the glass as half full," thing. "Count your blessings," she'd say. "Look on the bright side." And April's personal favorite, "It could be worse." Although heaven knew there were times, when they'd been reduced to eating grilled cheese sandwiches and tomato soup five nights out of seven, when she'd spot the pawn ticket and realize her mother had hocked her engagement ring—again—that April wanted to shake the woman and yell, "How could it possibly be *worse?*"

Only she never had, partly because she knew Mama was doing her best, and partly because they'd never actually gone hungry. Came darn close, more times than April wanted to remember, but there'd always been food of some description on the table. And they'd always, somehow, climbed out of whatever hole her father had put them in. Occasionally they even went out to eat, if only to Denny's or Long John Silver's.

And eventually Mama got her engagement ring back for good.

So despite April's inclination as a kid to think her mother's irritatingly positive outlook was a lot of hooey, it'd somehow taken root in her own psyche. Maybe because they had always landed on their feet, maybe because despite everything her parents had never stopped loving each other, she didn't know. But now, as her gaze drifted away from her computer and out her office window to watch Patrick working alongside his men—literally, on his knees in the dirt, tamping down the earth around a freshly planted bush as he joked with Duane, one of his crew—that whole "count your blessings" refrain started up again in her head.

Because yesterday—just as a for instance—she'd heard him inquire after someone's mom, apparently recovering from gall bladder surgery; the day before that she'd noticed him hand a small wrapped package to another guy for his kid's birthday. Witnessed the way he listened to his crew and their obvious respect for him—real respect, not some deferential attitude because of his injuries. He was the first one there in the mornings and the last one to leave at night, but not until he checked in with April, gave her an update, asked if she had any questions, wanted any changes. For that, she should be—and was—more than grateful. Professionally, he'd filled her glass to overflowing, and she'd be delighted to sing Shaughnessy and Sons' praises to anyone who asked. Clearly the man was a decent human being who truly cared about others.

But he'd also stopped meeting her gaze during those update sessions, or giving her even a sliver of opportunity to steer the conversation away from pavers and gravel and green things. Oh, he'd nod and say Lili was fine, when she asked, maybe even share an anecdote or two—he was a proud papa, after all—but beyond that, nada.

And frankly, she thought as she slammed shut her laptop lid and slipped her blazer over her cotton tunic, his continued reticence was getting on her last nerve.

April picked up the check she'd written earlier and let herself out onto the porch, shivering in the sudden chill. It'd been bizarrely warm these past few days, but the minute the sun went down, so did the temperature. Over by his truck, Patrick glanced up and spotted her, giving her a nod before crashing shut the tailgate. Muscles bulging underneath his long-sleeved Henley, he shrugged into his canvas work coat as he started toward her, juggling his clipboard from hand to hand as he walked. It wasn't a particularly graceful gait, but it was solid, the stride of a man who knew what he was about.

Or at least wanted the world to believe.

Before he even reached the steps, Patrick saw April hold out something. A check, looked like. "Your next payment," she said, her voice as crisp as the evening breeze.

Patrick looked at it, frowning. "Not due 'til tomorrow—"

"I know. But this way you can deposit it first thing. So here."

Eyes still on the check, he took it, a half smile denting the unscarred side of his face as he clamped it to the board. Never mind that the bank didn't open until after he would've been here an hour. "Thanks." Then he turned, scanning the yard. "So. You still good with everything?"

"Your work? Couldn't be happier. You? Not so much."

He didn't turn back. Not right away. Partly because the annoyance in her voice caught him up short, partly because he had a pretty good feeling he wasn't going to like what came next. Whatever that was. He'd forgotten how women wanted things spelled out, even when there weren't enough letters to do that.

But eventually he did, finally doing the one thing he'd refused to let himself do these past few days: look straight at her. He'd hoped she wouldn't notice. Or if she did, wouldn't care. Wrong on both counts, apparently.

"Not sure I understand," he said, which was true enough.

She crossed her arms, as a strange—and strangely arousing—combination of hurt and mad duked it out in her eyes. "Did I do something to tick you off?" she said, and he heard himself say, "You really want to have this conversation?" and over the sound of his words detonating in his head she lobbed back, "Implying that there's something to have a conversation about?" and longing and anger collided in his gut in a spectacular explosion.

Obviously trying to ignore this…this *buzzing* between them wasn't working. For either of them. At which point it occurred to him that, sometimes, in order to do the right thing, you had to be the bad guy. Whatever was going on underneath all that soft, silky, sunset-colored hair, it needed to be stopped, now.

So Patrick climbed the steps, watching her eyes pop wide open when he grabbed her left hand and gave it a little shake, a hundred colors flashing in the faceted stones, even in the waning light. "Why are you still wearing these?"

"What?" she squeaked out, frozen.

"Blythe told me you're a widow."

Mouth open, April snatched back her hand, holding it to her chest. "I wasn't trying to keep it a secret."

"Then why—?"

"For heaven's sake, Patrick—plenty of widows still wear their rings! What's the big deal?"

"How about because people might assume you're still married? Or at least, still *feel* married?" He crossed his arms. "Both of which seriously conflict with the messages you're sending out."

Color bloomed in her cheeks. "Messages?"

"Yeah, messages. Specifically of a 'let's get cozy' nature."

She blinked. "I don't—"

"Like hell. You don't really expect me to believe you have no idea how you've been looking at me?" He stepped closer, deliberately towering over her, ignoring the lust rearing its ugly, insistent head when he got a good whiff of her perfume. At how the breeze sifted through her hair, across her slender, very pink neck. God, that hair drove him crazy. Almost as crazy as that prissy little blue headband holding it off her face. "That I wouldn't pick up on it?"

Then she seemed to regroup, thrusting her hands into her jacket pockets and looking him smack in the eye, even though her voice shook. Barely, but it shook. "I was *going* to say, no, I don't still feel married. Not that it's any of your business, but—"

"What?"

"The rings…I've never owned anything this pretty in my life, okay? So maybe I just wasn't ready to chuck them into a safe, never to be seen again. And anyway, you don't think I noticed you looking at *me* exactly the same way?" Her eyes narrowed. "Even when you thought I *was* married?"

Busted.

"Fine. So I noticed you were hot. And my skills at keeping my thoughts under wraps might be a bit rusty. But that's all they were. Thoughts. Doesn't mean I had any intention of acting on 'em."

That soft-looking little mouth curved at the corners. "Before or after you found out I was single?"

"Either. Both. And damn it, you're doing it again, aren't you?"

Another blush washed over her cheeks. "Not intentionally—"

"You're barking up the wrong tree, April. Hell, you're not even in the right forest."

"I wasn't barking, for heaven's sake! I was just…looking—"

"Well, don't. Because I'm bad news. And for God's sake I don't need some gal taking pity on me, wondering what it would be like to shag the freak."

Brittle silence stretched between them, pierced only by a hawk's cry from behind the house. At last April opened her mouth. Shut it. Opened it again and said, "You honestly think that?"

"Yep."

"Then you're an idiot," she said, before she stomped back inside, the door slamming shut behind her.

Weirdly, Patrick didn't feel nearly as good about that as he'd expected to.

"Done," Blythe said, arms outstretched, her six-inch feather earrings a blur. "Done, done, done, done, *done*." Then she did a strange little NordicTrack shuffle in her stiletto booties that made April laugh, despite still feeling like fish doody several days after telling Patrick he was an idiot. Not that he wasn't. She just felt bad about it.

Panting a little, Blythe slung one slender arm around April's shoulders, surveying the finished gathering room. "You ready for this, sweetie?"

April crossed her arms over her lambswool turtleneck

and grinned, despite the trembling in her midsection. "I am so ready."

"Then let's kidnap Mel, go to Emerson's for lunch to celebrate."

"You're on."

Her cousin strode off to get her things from the office, leaving April to revel. Absorb. Minutes before, they'd finished the final walk-through of the upstairs, the five bedrooms outfitted in a combination of antiques, repurposed pieces salvaged from their grandmother's "collections," and funky yard-sale finds. Windows sparkled, bathrooms gleamed, deeply piled rugs invited bare toes to squish.

Yet April couldn't shake the feeling that any minute she was going to tumble out of bed and realize it'd all been a dream. But it wasn't. In fact, she'd been stupefied that morning to check the website and discover several booking requests for the festival, more for after the holidays. And she had to hire more staff and find a laundry service, set up accounts with various suppliers—

It was happening. It was really, really happening.

So this whole business with Patrick still hanging over her like a toxic cloud was patently unfair. He and his band of merry men—and two women—had finished up the day before as well, aside from the spring planting. She'd also paid for a year's worth of monthly maintenance, so she'd never have to think about keeping it all pretty, they'd do it for her. But now that the bulk of the job was done—and since she seriously doubted Patrick was going to show up in May, clippers in hand, to trim her topiaries—in theory she supposed she never had to think about him again, either. Let alone see him.

In a town the size of a peanut? Right.

"I texted Mel," Blythe said, wrapping a long, silver-threaded scarf around her neck as she emerged from the kitchen, the fringed ends gracefully blending into the folds of her cashmere cape. "She's going to meet us there."

"Excellent."

November had returned with a vengeance, making both women scurry out to Blythe's Prius, complete with a vanity plate that read WOWFCTR.

"I've been meaning to ask," Blythe said as April buckled her seat belt. "You ever change your mother's mind about coming up for Thanksgiving?"

"Hah. Only way that'll happen is if I blindfold her and toss her in a sack." The Prius silently navigated the circular drive and out onto the road leading through the gently worn neighborhood of rambling, multistory houses set on spacious lots, the bare-branched elms and maples and oaks seeming to scrape the cloudless, brilliant blue sky. April frowned over at her cousin. "Does your mom still have issues about Nana?"

Blythe darted a look in April's direction, then shrugged. "I have no idea. Not something we discussed." They passed a small farm, the flat, open field choked with Canada geese foraging for harvest leavings. "But you know, our grandmother made her own bed, pushing her daughters away."

"True, I suppose."

"So you'll go back to Richmond for the holiday?"

"Maybe. Haven't decided yet."

"You're welcome to hang with me. Or I'm sure Mel—"

"Thanks. But I probably will spend it with my folks."

Actually, she had no intention of going to Richmond—which she'd already told her mother, who'd then said they were having dinner with friends anyway. Just as well, being as April had realized that since this would be the first holiday without Clayton and his mother, she simply wanted some space to absorb that. And heaven knew she didn't want to spend it with Mel, since for one thing even though

April adored Ryder—whom Mel had loved from the time she was a little girl, and who was the main reason she'd returned to St. Mary's after swearing six ways to Sunday she never would—all that bliss was hard to take in a confined space. And for another Ryder's parents and Mel were still working out their own issues with each other, fallout from yet more of her grandmother's madness. Best to stay well away from that for a while—

"So. What's going on between you and Patrick?"

"What? Nothing—"

"No, if *nothing* was going on, he wouldn't have kept asking me questions the past couple days that he should've been asking you. Honestly, I leave town for one day, and it all goes to pot."

April frowned at her. "Excuse me?"

Her cousin pushed out a why-me? sigh. "You're single, he's single. You're young and adorable. He's young and sexy as hell. No chatter than I can tell that he's seeing anyone, no evidence that his injuries affected his testosterone level—"

"Blythe, jeez—"

"And I'm guessing you haven't been secretly getting it on with anybody, either, since Clayton's death."

Heat seared April's cheeks. "You don't have to be so… matter-of-fact about it."

"About what? That your husband is dead? And you're not? That you're only twenty-freaking-six years old, your husband has been gone for, what? Nearly a year? And you're still wearing your wedding rings even though—even though," she said when April opened her mouth, "you're looking at your landscaper like you've been on Atkins for a year and he's a Krispy Kreme donut. So, yeah. I'm matter-of-fact. Because somebody has to be, and apparently that's not you."

April gawked at her. "This from the woman who thinks, and I quote, that 'romance is a load of horse pucky'?"

Blythe snickered. "That's not exactly quoting me. And that applied to me. Not the rest of the world."

"Isn't that being a trifle hypocritical?"

"Ask me if I care."

Gravel crunched as she steered the car into the restaurant lot. Not a huge crowd, this time of year. During the summer, though, hour-long waits for tables at the seafood joint that always smelled of French fries, hush puppies and heaven were not uncommon. They spotted Mel's car, parked close to the wide plank leading to the pylon-supported building.

A chill traipsed up April's spine. "Oh, Lord—you've been discussing this with Mel, haven't you?"

"Hellz, yeah."

"So is this lunch? Or an intervention?"

Blythe cut the engine, grabbed her purse and grinned at April, all smokey-eyed devil woman. "Who says it can't be both?"

April groaned.

"You interested in Patrick or not?"

"Whether I am or not has nothing to do with—"

"Just answer the question."

So here it was. Moment of truth and all that. Even if it was little more than a formality, since if she hadn't been interested she wouldn't be obsessing like she was.

Blythe tapped the steering wheel. "Clock's ticking, sweetie."

"How about…intrigued?"

"Close enough," Blythe said, then patted April's knee. "Oh, c'mon…it'll be fun."

"For *you*," April muttered. Blythe chuckled.

Except the thing was, maybe she did need an intervention. Or at least a sounding board. Or two. Something her cousins had excelled at when April was fourteen, and they'd been only too willing to help her with her boy problems. They should only know how little progress, actually, she'd made on that particular front in the intervening years.

Although, if this went down the way she suspected it would, they were about to find out.

Chapter Four

April couldn't quite tell whose mouth was hanging farther open, although she gave the edge to Blythe.

"Get *out*. You're still a *virgin?*"

"Yep."

Okay, so she hadn't really meant to lead with the punch line, except her cousins had overwhelmed her with all this *advice,* and it sort of…popped out.

They exchanged flummoxed glances, then Mel frowned at her. "But you were—"

"Married. I know."

And Patrick thought *he* was the freak. Heh.

"So, see…" April frowned at her overstuffed shrimp salad sandwich, wondering how she was going to pick it up without half of it plopping back on the plate. "I really don't have a whole lot of experience. Or any, really. When it comes to, you know…"

"Seduction?" Blythe offered—kindly, it should be noted—and April's eyes shot to hers.

"Oops," Mel muttered, her pink hoodie clashing with the maroon vinyl booth seat. "Deer in headlights, straight ahead."

"I hadn't exactly thought of it like that," April said, finally picking up the bulging sandwich. *Plop.* She scooped up an escaped shrimp and bit into it. "But I guess I have to start somewhere."

Both women were still staring at her, absolutely still except for their chewing mouths. April sighed.

"My marriage..." She devoured another shrimp. "It wasn't about romance. Clayton and I were doing each other a favor."

"As opposed to doing each other," Blythe said, and Mel swatted her.

"I know, it sounds weird—"

"You think?"

"For God's sake, Blythe," Mel said, "will you shut up and let the girl tell the story?"

As in, the whole story. Instead of the uber-edited version she'd offered when they'd first reconnected in September, when she wasn't sure how her cousins would react to something that still sounded surreal, even to her.

"Okay," she said on a breath, then met their dual gazes. "Five years ago an agency in Richmond sent me to interview for a companion position to Clayton's mother, Helene, who lived with him. Which was bizarre in itself, since I have no idea why the agency thought I'd be a good fit. But I'd had so many rotten jobs by that point—" already privy to her sketchy childhood and her father's predilection for pipe dreams, her cousins nodded in sympathy "—that this one sounded too good to be true. It didn't require any real skills, which I didn't have, anyway. And it paid well." She blushed. "*Really* well. And Clayton was desperate, since the old gal had run off no less than six companions in the previous year."

Mel's eyes widened. "He told you that?"

"No. She did. Within a minute of meeting me."

"Sounds like a peach."

"But that's the thing—we hit it off right away. Not sure why—maybe because she reminded me of Nana, rattling around in her big old house. So there was nothing she could do or say I hadn't seen or heard before. I stood up to her, I guess. Wouldn't take her guff." She smiled, remembering. "Within a week, she was making faces when it was time for me to leave. Clay was her only child, and had never married, and I think she thought of me as the granddaughter she never had."

Blythe forked in a bite of her lobster salad. "So you tamed the beast?"

April laughed. "Not hardly. Old gal was a pain in the butt until the day she died." She sighed. "Six weeks after Clay did. I knew how to deal with her, is all. Clay was stunned." She felt a smile warm her insides. "And very, very grateful."

"So...?" Blythe gently prodded, buttering a homemade cheese biscuit.

April let her gaze drift outside, to the marina beyond the restaurant, the tethered boats gently bobbing in the slate blue water. "Clay and I would chat, when he was around. Mostly about his mother, at first. But then about other things. Movies, the news, whatever popped into our heads. And...it was nice. Not what I expected."

She looked back at her cousins. "A few months in, he asked if I'd consider living there full-time. In my own suite. Sitting room, fireplace, jetted tub, the works. And with a very hefty salary hike, to boot. I'd've been an idiot to refuse. And once I moved in, he and I started spending more time together, when he wasn't away on business. Didn't take long before I realized he was one of the kindest men I'd ever met. Very fair. And funny, in his own way. Even though he was a lot older than I was. And I liked him. Quite a bit, actually."

"Define 'a lot.'"

"In his forties."

Mel frowned. "And you weren't dating guys your own age?"

"My own age? As in, their early twenties?"

Blythe snorted. "Good point."

"I'd never dated much as it was. Even after we all stopped coming here for the summer. Besides, between school and working there wasn't any time. And anyway, the Rosses kept me plenty busy." She grinned. "They even took me to Europe with them. Ladies, I have seen Paris, and it is everything it's cracked up to be."

"And Clayton…" Mel said, munching a fried clam. "No girlfriends?"

"Helene said something about a fiancée years before, but I guess it never panned out. And he certainly never seemed…" She hesitated. "Interested." In front of her, two sets of eyebrows raised, and April sighed. "Yeah. Although I never knew for sure if he was gay. And this is all hindsight, anyway. Also not my point."

Her sandwich somehow finished, April wiped her fingers on her napkin, then tucked it under the rim of her plate. "Shortly after we got back, Daddy came down with some weird infection that nearly killed him. My parents had no insurance, and even though he pulled through, it was a long recuperation. And only Mama to take care of him. I nearly worried *myself* sick, wondering how we were going to pay the medical bills, if he'd have a relapse and we'd lose him altogether, about how hard this all was on

Mama. But I couldn't quit work to help her, since by then my income was all we had."

"Oh, honey..." Mel reached across the table for her hand. "I had no idea things were that bad."

"Nobody did. Mama didn't want the family to know, because then it would get back to Nana and she couldn't deal with the 'I told you sos.' About her marrying Daddy to begin with, I mean."

Blythe sighed. "And she would have, too."

"Yeah," April said. "Anyway, I tried to keep it together when I was around the Rosses, not let on what we were going through, but that's kind of hard to do when you're living in someone's house. Especially when your employer walks in on you when you're crying your eyes out."

"Oops," Mel said, and April smiled.

"I blurted out the whole sad story. And Clay simply... listened. And within the day..." Her throat got so tight she could barely speak. "He'd settled all their bills, arranged for a monthly stipend for them while my father was recuperating, and a nurse's aide to come in every day so Mama could get a break."

"Holy cannoli," Mel breathed. "That's like..." She slammed her chin into her hand. "Wow."

"I know. He said, after the miracle I'd worked with his mother, it was the least he could do. Then a month later he found out *he* was sick. But in his case, it was terminal. He told me, but he didn't want his mother to know. Not yet. I didn't think it was right, not telling her, but of course I said I wouldn't." She released a breath. "Less than a year, they'd given him. Poor man...he'd been knocked on his pins. He was quiet and reserved, but he took such a simple joy in life, in everything it had to offer, you know? Then he knocked *me* into next week by asking if I'd consider marrying him, saying how happy it would make Helene, especially since he knew how fond she was of me."

Her eyes glanced off first Mel's, then Blythe's. "After everything he'd done for my parents—and me," she said softly, "how could I say no?"

The waitress came over, asked if they wanted dessert. Blythe and April said no, they were good, but Mel ordered a piece of strawberry chiffon pie as big as her head. Which the waitress served with three forks.

Mel duly distributed the utensils, pushing the pie into the center of the table for easier access. No fool, she. "You didn't even consider refusing?"

April took a tiny forkful of the airy dessert, letting the tart sweetness melt on her tongue before she said, "I was shocked, of course, but...no. I cared for them both too much. He also promised," she said softly, "that I'd never have to worry about my parents' finances again."

Fork halfway to her mouth, Blythe frowned. "But you were married for nearly four years."

"I know. His oncologist was incredulous. Especially since Clay refused any aggressive treatment. In fact for a while he was even well enough to do some more traveling."

"And you never...?"

April swiped another tiny bite that blurred as her eyes swam with tears. "Even if he could have...that wasn't what we had."

"But was it what you wanted?"

"I suppose I didn't let myself think about it."

Blythe took the last bite of pie. Mel signaled for another piece. "But...four years...? Wow."

A tight smile tugged at April's mouth. "Oh, when Clay realized he apparently wasn't leaving on the doctors' schedule, he asked me if I wanted to reconsider our arrangement. Several times. With the understanding that he'd keep his end of the agreement. About my parents, I mean. But each time I told him no."

"Because of everything he'd done for you?"

April thought about that for a moment. "I'm not going to say that wasn't part of it. Aside from that, though, I'd also made a promise, of my own free will. And I'm not one to back out of something simply because it gets hard. Or inconvenient. But the real reason I stayed was because I loved him. Loved them both. They were very dear friends, and I wouldn't have turned my back on either of them for the world. And what other people think about that...well, it's really none of their concern, is it?"

She saw tears bunch in the corners of Mel's eyes. "No. It sure as hell isn't. Even so—" those eyes narrowed "—Blythe and I aren't 'other people.' And keeping secrets is for the birds. It's kind of hard to get your back if you don't let us see it. Am I right?" she said to Blythe, who muttered something that sounded like "Sure thing," as the second piece of pie came.

They all picked up their forks again and dived in, munching for several seconds before Blythe said to April, "And you really, truly never found anyone before you met Clayton you wanted to get naked with?"

"Good Lord, Blythe," Mel said, "give it a rest."

"No, it's okay." April looked Blythe in the eye. "I was hardly the only twenty-one-year-old virgin out there."

"One of the few. If not proud," Blythe said, and Mel smacked her again.

April shrugged. "First off, that's none of anybody's business, either. Secondly, this chick does not cast her pearls before swine, thank you very much," which led Mel to mumble something about wishing somebody had said that to her, back in the day. Although, Blythe then pointed out, at least Mel's pearls-before-swine experience had resulted in the smartest, most awesome ten-year-old girl, ever, so it all worked out, before swinging her gaze back to April.

"Only now you're twenty-six. And I take it Patrick's not swine."

April stuffed another bite of pie into her mouth. Thought about how he interacted with Lili. His crew. His lame attempt at scaring her. "No," she said, very softly.

"Then what are you waiting for? Get out there and cast those pearls, girl!"

"Except you forget I have no idea how to go about that," April said, right about the same time Mel poked Blythe again, this time nodding toward the restaurant's entrance. Which April couldn't see because she had her back to it.

"Tell me he just walked in."

"Yep." Mel thrust out her hand. "Rings off. Now. Before he spots us."

"What? I can't—"

"You can. And you will. Can't cast the pearls while you're still wearing the diamonds." She waggled her fingers. "They'll be perfectly safe, I promise. And you can have 'em back when…" Her eyes crinkled in thought. "When you score your first date."

"With Patrick?"

"With anybody. His brother's with him and he ain't half bad, either." She shrugged. "Options."

"This is very true," Blythe said. "They clearly breed them well, those Shaughnessys—"

"April!" Mel said under her breath. *"Now."*

"Okay, okay…" She twisted off the rings and handed them over, thinking, *There, done,* as April slipped them into a zippered compartment in her wallet, then her wallet back inside her purse.

Strange that anticipation should feel so much like panic. Especially when she heard voices coming closer, Patrick's brother's and the waitress's, mostly. Luke was a notorious flirt, if the stories were to be believed. The kind of man known to make women go all fluttery and stupid. Then, as she rubbed where her rings had been, she heard Patrick's rumbly voice, she shut her eyes, thinking, *Yeah. Like that*.

Then somebody kicked her under the table, making her yelp, forcing her to look up and smile at the Shaughnessy brothers, both dark-haired and blue-eyed, one grinning, one not. Only, in that instant, she saw the glower for what it was—or more to the point, what it wasn't—and her heart melted.

Let the games begin, she thought, and tossed out that first, all-important pearl.

Leave it to his dumbass brother to make a beeline for the cousins' table. Or more to the point, to take Patrick's muttered, "Not a good idea, bro," as a challenge. So here he was, standing in front of April with his hands shoved in his pockets without a clue what to say.

Not that this was a huge issue with Luke around, who'd been chatting up girls since the sixth grade. Yeah, the nuns had had their hands full with that one, boy.

But while Luke and Mel and Blythe were yakking away—about what, Patrick had no idea, he couldn't hear for the ringing in his ears—April fixed that soft, sweet gaze on him, smiling like they'd never had that last conversation. Like she hadn't told him he was an idiot.

Like he hadn't acted like one.

In the reflected light splashing through the window, her hair seemed redder, her eyes more turquoise. And although the cream-colored, fluffy sweater covered her from chin to wrists, it also clung to everything between. How she could look so hot and so innocent at the same time was beyond him, but it was a deadly combination, that was for damn sure.

The waitress brought them their check. Mel and Blythe scrapped over it like cats over a chicken bone, making Luke laugh and Patrick breathe a sigh of relief. A few minutes more, and they'd be gone.

"How's it going?" April said over the din.

"Okay," he said, making himself shrug. Avoiding her gaze.

"Business good?"

He squinted out the window at a sailboat in the open water beyond the marina, its white sails blinding against the blue sky. "Getting by."

"And Lili?"

The check folder clamped in her hand, Blythe rose from the table and gathered her purse, flirting with his brother in that way women did when they didn't mean it. And Luke was eating it up. Dumbass.

"Um...she's great," Patrick said, reluctantly returning his attention to April, who'd stood as well to wriggle into her blazer before hiking up her own purse onto her right shoulder.

With her left hand.

His gaze zinged to hers. Which she took captive with another one of those sweet smiles before following her cousins through the restaurant to the cashier. And never looking back.

"Y'all want to sit here?" Jeannie, the waitress, asked. "I can clean it up in a jiff."

"Sure," Luke said, sliding behind the table and inhaling deeply. "Smell that?"

Patrick hesitated, then sat across from him, scarred side to window, the seat still warm from April. "Besides the fried fish?" True to her word, the waitress cleaned off the table in a jiffy, laying down fresh paper napkins and cutlery, then menus. Superfluous though they were, since everybody in St. Mary's knew the menu by heart from the time they could talk. Probably before.

Luke breathed deeply again, then let out his breath on a happy sigh. "No, numskull. *Women.* Sweetest smell in the world."

Patrick shook his head. "You're pathetic."

"No, *you're* pathetic," Luke said, leaning back in the booth, his arm stretched across the back. "Give me one good reason why you haven't asked April out."

"And since when is my personal life any of your concern?"

Ignoring him, Luke sat forward again to tick off a list on his fingers. "She's cute, she's available and she's interested. And don't tell me she's not." Luke's sharp gaze softened. "And she seems like a real doll."

Jeannie brought them tea, flirted a little more, took their orders and left. "Which is precisely why she's not my type."

"Type? What the hell, *type?* All I'm saying is ask her out. See where it goes. Why are you looking under the table?"

"Checking to see if Ma's hiding under there." Patrick straightened. "'Cause that sure sounds like her words coming out of your mouth, Mr. Marriage Is For Suckers."

"Who's talking marriage, for crying out loud? I'm just saying, what's the harm in, you know? A little female companionship, if you get my drift."

"Yeah. Got it. Except April's not *that* type."

"Not *your* type, not *that* type…" Luke shook his head. "You're hopeless, you know that?"

"No, I'm a realist. For one thing, in case you missed it, I tried dating. It sucked. Or I suck at it, not sure which. For another, April's…classy. And real. Not that you'd know anything about that—"

"Hey!"

"She's also a recent widow."

"Oh, yeah? Then she's probably…how can I put this?" Luke grinned. "Needy."

"Just what *I* need."

"Actually—"

"In any case, I doubt she even knows what she wants right now. Or needs."

"Oh, and you do?" Luke leaned forward, lowering his voice. "There's worse things than having a fling with a hot widow, bro—"

"Luke. Stop it."

"Huh," Luke said, leaning back again.

Patrick's gaze shot to his brother's. "What?"

"You're scared."

"I'm not—"

"The hell you say. You're scared. And you know *why?* Because you've got feelings for her."

"That's ridiculous, I barely know her."

"And how many times have we heard Pop tell us about how, like, within five minutes of meeting Ma, he knew. Huh? How many times?"

Patrick rubbed his scarred cheek, the blood trying to come to the surface making the skin itch. "And since when do you believe in that crap?"

"Just because it hasn't happened for me doesn't mean it didn't for them. Or couldn't for anybody else." He gestured toward Patrick. "Like, say, you."

"And if you recall," Patrick said steadily, his gaze pinned to his brother's, "it did happen for me. With Natalie. And look how that turned out."

"And you two were how old when you met? Hell, at that

age everybody's The One. Until you see somebody else. Then she got pregnant, which only complicated things, right?"

"I did love Nat, Luke. And if…" This time the burn was inside, where it lurked like a pilot light, ready to ignite at a moment's notice.

"And if you hadn't gotten injured," Luke said, almost gently, "you'd still be together. Except you did, and you're not. And you know something? That's not your fault."

For the second time, Patrick flinched. Partly at his brother's words, but more because of the force behind them—a force strong enough to slash open the shroud of bitterness and self-pity Patrick hadn't even known was there. Or at least had been denying pretty damn hard.

He released a breath. "I'm being a butt, huh?"

"Nah. Okay, maybe a little," Luke said with another grin. "But the thing is, and what you apparently haven't taken into account, is that April already knows the worst, doesn't she? Your mug is never gonna look any better than it does now, you've got mood swings worse than a fourteen-year-old girl and enough baggage to sink an aircraft carrier. Yet somehow she *likes* you. And you're still finding excuses why hooking up with her is a bad idea?"

When Patrick glared at his brother, he shrugged. "Fine, word it however you want. *But*—" Luke leaned forward again "—one word, buddy. *Opportunity*. Maybe nothing will come of it, maybe not. But you sure as hell aren't happy with the way things are now, so what've you got to lose? You can't hide behind what happened forever. So ask her out." He pointed at him. "I dare you."

To a large extent, Patrick knew what his brother was saying was true. He couldn't deny that his resistance went contrary to everything he'd promised himself about not letting circumstances—or fear—limit him.

Even so, he thought as Jeannie brought them their food, it was one thing to face his own demons, another thing entirely to drag somebody else into the battle with him. And there was Lili to consider, too. So he wasn't exactly a free agent here....

"I'll think about it," he said, and his brother softly swore.

Thanksgiving Day had started out clear and sunny, but by midday a typical late-fall gloom had settled over the town, the roiling clouds occasionally spitting a cold, mournful rain across the inn's windows. Oddly, though, April didn't feel the least bit melancholy, despite being alone in the huge house. She had a fire going in the gathering room's retrofitted gas fireplace and all manner of leftover goodies in the fridge, from which she assembled a noontime dinner worthy of royalty. Then she plunked herself at one of the six deliberately mismatched tables in the dining room, watching the rain pummel the churning gray water beyond the pier as she ate and remembering her last Thanksgiving. With Clay.

Did that seem like a million years ago, or what?

Not feeling right about leaving him, she'd spent that Thanksgiving without her parents, too. They'd understood—they'd adored Clay. And April and Helene had taken their little meal—soup, April thought—with Clay in his room, eating off trays to keep him company.

Tears came to her eyes as the scene replayed in her mind. But not of sadness as much as gratitude, that she'd been there for both of them. That they'd left this world knowing they were loved. And that she'd had the privilege of loving them, too. Of their loving her.

Her meal finished, April carried her plate and tea glass back to the kitchen, washing them by hand even though there were two dishwashers—one in here and another in the butler's pantry—as the rain suddenly stopped, a sunbeam streaking across the warm maple floor. Smiling, April returned to the dining room to let herself out into the spiffed-up sunroom overlooking the grounds behind the house, the estuary beyond. The room was all white—wooden floor, slivers of beadboarded wall between the windows, the wicker furniture—except for the sisal rugs and bright floral cushions that would eventually mimic the dozens of rose bushes Patrick and his crew had planted outside.

She still couldn't get over how amazing it all was. Couldn't wait to book the inn's first wedding. Already she envisioned the rows of white chairs, the gazebo or chuppah entwined with garlands, the beaming couple exchanging their vows underneath....

Even though the ground was soaked, and her thin cardigan no match for the cold, the sun lured her outside, even as her thoughts lured her along paths that, if she had any sense, she wouldn't go down. Although it'd felt unaccountably good, knowing she'd thrown Patrick at Emerson's, both by playing it cool—go, her—and by making sure he noticed she'd ditched her rings. The look on his face? Priceless. And endearing, in a bizarre sort of way.

Speaking of the rings, Mel had assured her they were safe—from any temptation April might have to put them back on, especially. It felt weird, not wearing them, but... freeing, too.

But what was *really* freeing was finally finding the guts to shuck off those doubts and scruples and plunge bare naked into possibility. Emotional skinny-dipping, she thought, chuckling. Patrick was a good man. And obviously a great father. If the prospect of seeing where this led was a little scary...well. She was hardly a stranger to scary, was she?

The black cloud mushroomed out of nowhere, the wind charging her like a ferocious beast and turning even the tiniest twigs into brutal missiles. Her cardigan yanked over her face against the assault, April staggered across the grass and back inside, wrestling shut the door behind her.

Holy cow. The storm had returned with a vengeance, ripping through the yard, hurtling against the house as though desperate to get inside. Lights flickered as April bolted through the kitchen, keeping well away from the windows, even though she knew they were stormworthy. As was the house, which had withstood its share of hurricanes.

Still. Couldn't hurt to wait things out in the cellar. A flashlight snatched from a shelf by the door, she ran down into the old boiler room, trying not to give her imagination its head. Lord, she'd never felt so alone in her life. Or more helpless. Extremely annoying, that.

Then the wind stopped, *boom,* as though a switch had been flipped. April waited, the sweater clutched to her thudding heart, listening to her own breathing in the sudden, almost eerie calm. Until, through a small window near the cellar ceiling, she saw sunlight.

Well, that had been weird.

She tiptoed upstairs, replacing the flashlight before cautiously approaching one of the kitchen windows—

Oh, dear God.

April froze, then spun around and ran to the front of the house, swinging open the front door.

Hand over her mouth and tears welling in her eyes at the sight in front of her, she crept out onto the front porch and sank onto the top step, totally oblivious to the sheen of ice-cold water glazing the freshly painted boards.

Chapter Five

The scents of cinnamon and roasting turkey, six different perfumes and at least one poopy baby, swarmed Patrick as he walked into his parents' house on Thanksgiving. Lili perched on his hip, he dodged a screeching, undulating clot of small people on his way back to the kitchen. Every year the holidays got crazier. And more crowded. And louder. Not that his married siblings with larger houses hadn't suggested rotating the hosting duties, but since Ma found the very thought appalling, they kept cramming an ever-increasing number of bodies into the tiny foursquare.

Never mind it'd been years since they'd all been able to sit together. Or that, every year, Ma bitched about finding squashed pumpkin pie in the sofa cushions, or that a kid or two got temporarily misplaced. Holidays meant home, and home meant where you grew up. Where your parents still lived.

And that was that.

"There's my sweetie pie!" Ma said over the din of five women in a kitchen that barely fit one. Her hands gooped up with whatever she was making, she leaned forward so Patrick could swing—carefully—Lili over for a kiss. "Put her down, let her go play with the cousins." The kid let loose, his mother returned to her stirring, giving Patrick a quick smile.

"So Luke tells me—"

"Ma!" Frances, his oldest sister, yelled from the other side of the kitchen. "Where's the kosher salt?"

"I have no idea, use the regular stuff, it's right in that cupboard in front of you. And don't you dare go anywhere," she said to Patrick, "I want to talk to you—"

"Grams!" A bright-eyed rug rat popped up between them. "Poppa says the game's on, are there any munchies?"

"Yeah. It's called Thanksgiving dinner. And he can cool his jets for an hour until it's done." The same argument they had every year. Tradition. Ma swiped her hand across her butt, then grabbed the kid's chin. "You got all that?"

"Uh-huh," the kid said, and disappeared.

"An hour, huh?"

"Got the turkey in a little late, there's no juices in the pan yet. So it's gonna be a while. Anyway, so your brother—"

"Holy cow," Sarah, his youngest sister, said, staring at the small flat-screen TV mounted where the bulletin board used to be. "A small tornado touched down north of town?"

Patrick's head jerked around. "What?"

"Yeah. Look."

He edged past assorted bosoms, frowning at the news crawl at the bottom of the screen. North would be—

Ignoring his mother's, "Where are you going, I'm not done with you!" Patrick pushed through the crush and through the back door, onto the faded deck his father had built twenty years before. Seconds later he was down in the bare, brown yard, his cell clamped to his ear. "C'mon, c'mon...answer, dammit."

No response.

She was probably fine. Probably not even there, maybe with her folks in Richmond. Or with Mel and Ryder—

Staring at the tangle of dead vines in his mother's barren vegetable patch, he banged the phone three times against his thigh, then called again. Still no answer.

"Uh...yeah..." He palmed his freezing head. "It's Patrick. The, uh, news said maybe a tornado touched down around there, so, um, just checking to make sure you're okay. Call if you want."

Holy crap...he was *shaking*?

He sure as hell was. And you know what? If dinner was an hour out, what could it hurt to swing by the inn for a minute?

"Patrick?"

He looked up, saw Ma watching him from the deck, hugging herself against the chill.

"Tell Lili I'll be back in a little bit," he said, then strode off through the side gate before his mother could ask why.

Although, after he'd driven a few miles through the obviously untouched countryside, he started to feel stupid. Wasn't like the media never exaggerated or anything. Especially about the weather—

It was subtle, at first. A tree branch by the side of the road. A chewed-up shingle, followed by three or four. Then, as he got within a half mile of the inn, things got more serious—a fifty-foot pine, toppled in someone's front yard; a missing restaurant sign; a crumpled metal shed smashed into the side of a building. Whatever it was, it'd been mean enough to screw up a lot of Thanksgivings.

His chest tight, Patrick approached the inn, only to let

out a choice cuss word when he saw the mangled front yard. House seemed okay, from what he could tell, but…

Hell, did April even know? He jerked the truck into the parking area and jumped out, not bothering to shut the door before making tracks across the yard, up the porch steps.

"April! *April!*" He pounded on the door, rang the bell. Pounded again. "You in there?"

No answer.

His heart racing, he skipped back down the stairs, then turned, looking up at the house. Now he could see a couple shutters missing or knocked askew, some of the gutter ripped off. Nothing major, though. At least.

He forced himself to look at the front yard again. Okay, yeah, it was a mess, but not irreparable. Didn't even look like anything was missing, although there were tree limbs and such from other people's yards. Calmer now, he took off around the side of the house, past the bank of rhododendrons he'd planted against the new siding. Wind must've come from the other direction, they looked fine. And maybe, if April was away, he and the guys could come out tomorrow, get most of it cleaned up before she returned—

He swore again when he reached the back. One of the old loblolly pines lay across what was left of the pulverized gazebo. Some of the new trees he'd planted, too, had been uprooted—

"Patrick?"

He swiveled, not sure whether to laugh or get mad when he saw April, filthy as hell and practically swallowed up in somebody's old sweatshirt and too-big rubber boots— but still with that headband, boy—dragging a tree branch three times longer than she was tall.

"What in the name of all that's holy are you doing?"

"Cleaning up my yard." He watched about a hundred

expressions cross that cute, filthy face. "What on earth are you doing here?"

To his chagrin, he felt his face heat to where it was almost painful. He couldn't decide what was worse, the jolt to his system when he didn't know if she was okay, or the one when he found out she was. Man, was he in deep crap or what? "You didn't get my voice mail?"

"What? Oh. No. I left my cell on the kitchen counter when I went outside—before the storm, I mean—and I guess I forgot it afterward." She dropped the branch, then scowled at it. "I was a little preoccupied."

"You were here? Alone?"

"Yeah." Facing him again, she stuffed her thumbs in her jeans' pockets. "Hid out in the cellar until it was over."

"Good call."

"I thought so."

"Were you scared?"

"It happened so fast, 'scared' didn't have time to kick in. And you haven't answered my—"

"It was on the news, they think it was a small tornado—"

Her eyes went wide as saucers. "You're kidding?"

"And I thought maybe I should check on...the place." He paused. "On you. *Are* you okay?"

"Just peachy," she muttered, then dragged the muddy glove across her cheek. "A tornado, huh?"

"They think. Once in a lifetime thing, most likely."

"True. Although..." Her gaze drifted out over the ransacked yard. "Oh, Lord, Patrick," she sighed out. "All that work y'all did..."

"That, we can fix—"

His cell rang. He dug it out of his pocket, grimacing at his brother's number.

"Dude," Luke said in his ear, "where are you? Ma said you took off, the turkey's about to come out of the oven—"

"I'm at April's," he said, turning away. "The storm…it was pretty bad. She's got a fifty-foot loblolly down, it took the gazebo with it—"

"Damn."

"And a lot of the plantings." He sighed. "Tell Ma I'm sorry, but I can't leave with everything all torn up like this. You pigs better save me some pie, though. I'll get it when I stop by later to pick up Lili. Okay?"

"Uh…sure, I'll tell her, but—"

He didn't mean to cut off his brother. Or maybe he did. But he turned back to find April watching him with a funny expression on her face.

"Tell me you're not missing Thanksgiving on account of some stupid old storm."

"Why not? You are."

"Actually, I had Thanksgiving already," she said, grabbing her tree branch again. Gritting her teeth.

"With your cousin? And for God's sake, put that down."

A beat or two passed before she dumped the branch, then tugged off one glove to cram her windblown hair behind one ear. He'd never seen her that messy. Or less inclined to care that she was. "No, by myself."

"As in, alone?"

"That's usually what 'by myself' means. Got a problem with that?"

Patrick looked at her for a moment, then tramped back to his truck to get a pair of gloves. Yanking them on, he tramped back, considering the branch. "Where was this headed?"

"I don't know. The road, I suppose. I thought if I could at least clear out the smaller stuff…" She turned away, clearing her throat. "One of the pines fell over. The gazebo…"

"I know. I saw. It's okay, we'll take care of it."

"I'll pay you—"

"Don't worry about it." He hefted the branch, carted it down one of the paths toward the road. Once everything was gathered, they could decide if they needed a dump truck or not. Although the pine could be cut up, turned into firewood maybe—

"Why are you being so nice to me?"

April had come up behind him, startling him. He turned. "What?"

"For somebody who told me the other day he's...what was that again? That you're 'bad news'?" Her eyes went all slitty. "Sorry, big guy, but the pieces don't add up."

He let their gazes tangle for a moment before spotting another branch a few feet away. "Don't read more into this than there is."

"Oh, no? You tried to make me think you're a jerk, Patrick. But a jerk..." The breeze made her shiver; she wrapped her arms around herself, keeping their gazes locked. "A jerk doesn't leave a holiday family dinner to come check up on a woman he'd done everything in his power to blow off."

Wordlessly, he hauled the second branch over, dumped it on top of the first. Stomped back into the yard to start assessing the damage, what could be saved, what would have to be replaced. "Don't take it personally," he said at last. "It's nothing I wouldn't've done for any other client." At her silence, he looked back. Her mouth was crooked up in another one of those weird little smiles. As she shook her head. "What now?"

"You are so full of it," she muttered, tugging her gloves back on.

She was so adorable he got a little dizzy for a moment. Which, considering, between the mud and the tangled hair and the disreputable state of her appearance in general that she looked like some street urchin, did not speak well of Patrick's mental state.

"So," she said, "game plan?"

Running like hell? "Pardon?"

"For the grounds?"

Right. He unhooked his gaze from hers, then pointed to the nearest bed. "We can probably save a lot of those plants by getting the debris off 'em before any real damage is done. So why don't you start with that?"

He stopped, staring down the street.

"What are you looking at?" April asked, swiveling to follow his gaze and shielding her eyes from the sun spearing through the leftover clouds. "Is that—?"

"It would appear so."

As, one by one, an assortment of Shaughnessy vehicles pulled up to meet them on the driveway, April turned to him, a mixture of disbelief and gratitude in her eyes. "You're all nuts."

That they were, Patrick thought as his family piled out of those vehicles, apparently bearing their entire Thanksgiving feast. Then a tight grin pulled at his mouth as his mother made a beeline for April.

And, short of tackling the woman and throwing her in the back of somebody's minivan, there wasn't a damn thing he could do about it.

It was like being swarmed by angels, April thought, too amazed to do more than watch the procession of gabbing women—and a slew of kids—tote platters and covered dishes and Crock-Pots past her and into the house. The menfolk had immediately manned their clippers and shovels and chainsaws, not only to tackle her yard, but two of them headed across the street to one of the neighbors who'd probably not been amused to find his forty-foot oak across his driveway.

"I hope you don't mind us barging in like this," Patrick's mother said after introducing herself, her clasp firm and warm. As was her smile, the smile of a woman who'd seen it all. And survived. "But when we found out how bad it was…"

Still holding April's hand, Kate scanned the front yard before looking at April again, her gaze sympathetic underneath steel-colored bangs. "We couldn't very well go on and enjoy our dinner now, could we? Knowing that you and our Patrick weren't." Finally she let go, her eyes crinkling when she laughed. "So we brought dinner here! We can eat whenever the guys are finished."

Tears swam in April's eyes, that these people would drop everything… "They even left their football?" she asked, remembering her mother always having to carefully time Thanksgiving dinner around whatever game was on.

Another laugh burst from Kate's lungs. "God bless DVR, right? But in any case, soon as Luke told them what had happened, they were on their feet, grabbing their coats. Because that's how my guys roll."

"Even so, I can't believe…" Her head wagging, April dropped onto the porch's top step, then lowered her face into her hands. Kate sat beside her, rubbing her back.

"It's okay, hon. We're here now, so don't you worry," she said, a trace of Ireland in her speech. "The boys will soon set it all to rights. Although I've lived here all my life, never saw the like. A freak occurrence, for sure."

On a little laugh, April let her hands fall, her gaze latching like a heat-seeking missile on to Patrick, sawing branches with Luke and his dad at the edge of the yard. "Sometimes, I feel like my entire life is a series of freak occurrences."

"And don't I hear you on that," Kate said on a light chuckle, giving April's shoulder a squeeze before letting go to fold her hands together. Patrick's mother was dressed like the rest of the family, in jeans and heavy-duty sneakers, although in her case a bit of a turquoise sweater peeked out from behind her open car coat. No standing on ceremony with this crowd.

Although still feeling more than a trifle overwhelmed, April finally remembered her manners. "Thank you."

"You're more than welcome. We're only glad we can help." Then she laughed. "As long as those doofuses get fed," she said, nodding toward the men, "they're happy."

April blew out a breath, then started to rise. "Speaking of which, I should probably go help in the kitchen."

"With that lot? I'd say you're much safer staying out of their way. Although Patrick tells me the kitchen is the stuff dreams are made of?"

"It is," April said, sitting again. "At least, my cousin Mel—the one who's going to be the inn's main chef— tells me it is." She pulled a face. "I can barely make toast. But are you sure you want to stay out here? It's kind of chilly—"

"Oh, don't mind about me, love, I'm fine." Glancing back at the house over her shoulder, she sighed. "Joe and I were married here, you know."

"You were?"

"Yeah. So I have a special place in my heart for the house, as you can imagine." She smiled at April. "I'm so glad you decided to reopen it."

"Me, too."

A pause preceded, "Patrick tells me you're a widow?"

A question that by rights shouldn't make her uncomfortable. It was, after all, a fact. But as kindly as the question was asked, the skin between April's shoulder blades still prickled. "I am. For almost a year now. So who is everybody?" she said, diverting the conversation while she still could and not appear rude. "I know Patrick's dad, and Luke, but the others?"

One by one, Kate pointed them out, from her oldest, Joe Junior, to "baby" Sean, a beanpole in a beanie and the only one of the four boys, she said, completely uninterested in going into the family business.

"A lawyer, he wants to be," Kate with a shrug. And a proud smile. There were others, as well—her youngest daughter's boyfriend, a striking young black man, who like Sarah was studying for his masters at U of M; her oldest daughter Frannie's husband, blond and bulky, whose laugh could be heard to Chincoteague; and the Rocky-era Sly Stallone lookalike married to her middle daughter Bree. They all had names, of course, but by the fourth or fifth they'd all become swirled together—

She caught Patrick looking over at her and his mother. Not glowering, exactly, but close.

"Oh, dear," Kate said. "Someone's not happy with me."

"You?" April frowned at Patrick's mother. "Why you?"

"Because I've got you all to myself," she said with a little shrug. "He's seen me do this before, of course. With the others."

"Seen you do what bef—?" The light dawned. "Oh." She sighed. "Mrs. Shaughnessy—"

"Kate. Please."

"Kate—"

"I'm not trying to matchmake, believe it or not. Or stir up trouble, contrary to what Patrick is probably thinking right now. But siblings tattle. And Luke told me about the exchange between the two of you at Emerson's the other day."

April's heart bumped. "Exchange? We hardly said a dozen words to each other."

"So Luke said," Kate said, smiling, and April turned aside, blushing. Kate chuckled. "I like to think I'm a wise old hen who's learned a thing or two from watching her chicks fall in and out of love more times than I can count. And I'm seeing very clear signs that Patrick's...interested. And mad as hell, too, because he doesn't know what to do about it. About you."

"But...there's nothing going on between us."

"Yet."

Suddenly all those yakking women and kids in her kitchen sounded appealing. Then again, if anybody understood the man, it would be his mama. She'd only have his best interest at heart, too. Especially after—

"I'm sorry," his mother gently said. "I'm making you uncomfortable."

"You're not," April said after a moment. "The conversation is. However..." She deliberately stared at Patrick until he turned her way again. Glowered again. Looked away again. "Luke wasn't imagining things," she said. "At least on my end. Because I'm interested, too. Especially since I can tell Patrick's trying to keep his distance. Except what he says and how he acts are two different things."

"He's been hurt, love," his mother said gently. "And I'm not talking about what he's gone through physically, although naturally that's been no small challenge."

"What happened?" April asked, her gaze steady on Patrick.

"You don't know?" When April shook her head, Kate sighed. "Not that this is a surprise. He hates when people fuss over him. Make a big deal out of it."

April's eyes cut to Kate's profile. "A big deal out of what?"

"He was in Iraq," she said softly. "In the army, nearing the end of his tour of duty four years ago. A bomb went off in a house shortly after he and his team entered, setting it on fire." Her voice softened. "Two of those men owe their lives to him."

"And...the others?" April whispered.

Kate shook her head. Her eyes stinging, April reached for his mother's hand, the older woman's fingers closing around hers in silent understanding. "We're incredibly proud of him for everything he's overcome thus far. And I know there's been plenty of times when he's wanted to give up. Especially when he finally came home—back to his wife and child, I mean—and she told him she couldn't..."

Kate stopped, clearly choked up. "Men hear all their lives that they have to be strong. That they're not allowed to hurt, or to hide it if they are. So they—the men—get frustrated and confused and pull away when all they want is to be comforted."

April realized Kate was squeezing her hand. "Patrick won't let you comfort him?"

She was quiet for a moment, "I think I was afraid to try. That *he'd* think I was treating him like my baby." With a soft laugh she scrubbed away a tear with the edge of her sweater sleeve.

"Which of course he still is. They all are." Then she sighed. "Obviously he doesn't look the same. And I gather he still has nightmares, although not as often as before. He may be in therapy all his life, for both the physical and mental issues. But inside, past all the junk, he's no different than he ever was. Patrick was the happiest kid, always smiling, always goofing around."

"And you want to see that kid again."

The older woman dug a tissue out of her pocket, wiped her nose. "Yes." She stopped again, clearing her throat.

"Patrick needs someone in his life—besides us, I mean—with the strength and courage to know what's true about him even when things are tough. To comfort him even when he says he doesn't want it. To, I don't know, coax who he used to be out of hiding. Natalie—his ex—wasn't that person."

April almost laughed. "And you think I am?"

"Oh, I have no idea. I've just met you. But *you* need to know what you're getting yourself into. If things were to… progress. For both your sakes—"

"Ma!" A big-boned redhead who looked very much like Kate stuck her head out the front door. "You want to make the gravy, or you want me to?"

"I'll be right there, Frannie." Kate got to her feet, dusting off her bottom and stretching a little. "Old butts and hard steps don't mix," she said on a laugh as April stood as well, flinching slightly when Kate drew her into a hard hug, whispering, "Knowledge is power," before heading into the house.

April followed Patrick's mother inside, stopping for a moment in the lobby to process, if not steel herself against, the raucous laughter drifting out from the kitchen. A vociferous bunch, those Shaughnessys.

Another woman appeared, this one a little younger than the first. Thinner. Wiry haired. "April, right? I'm Bree, another sister," she said, striding across the foyer to pump April's hand, a huge grin splitting her pretty face. "The house is seriously amazing. And the kitchen…" She laughed. "Oh. My. God." When April laughed back, Bree thumbed over her shoulder. "You mind if we rearrange the dining room furniture—?"

"Oh! No, go right ahead, do whatever you like with it."

"Got it." Bree disappeared, and April shut her eyes.

She'd originally envisioned the inn as a refuge from the

storm of life, perhaps because that's how she'd seen it as a child—an antidote to that constant upheaval. Not that she expected being an innkeeper would be all sunshine and roses, or that there would never be surprises—she grimaced, thinking of the ravaged grounds—but as much as lay within her power she wanted her guests to feel that same peace.

Except now she remembered how they'd laughed their way through those summers, she and Mel and Blythe, the walls of their grandmother's house ringing with their shrieks of glee. As had her grandmother's ears, most likely. Oh, there'd been no peace back then, she thought, smiling.

But there had been something even better:

Joy.

Excitement shuffled through her as she realized what had been before was still here, more than sufficient to trump the bitter memories her mother wanted to believe had infected the place. *That's* what had been at the root of that silly childhood dream of one day owning the Rinehart property, that had made her jump on the opportunity to buy out her cousins.

Another burst of laughter went up, this time from the dining room, along with the bumps and knocks and scraping of furniture being rearranged, and tears burned her eyes, happy tears, as she pictured all the weddings and anniversaries and family gatherings she hoped to host in the coming years. Then the men began trooping in, Patrick demanding they all remove their shoes, not touch anything until they'd washed their hands, and her heart warmed, then cramped, as she replayed his mother's words in her head.

Because being an adult was all well and good, but not at the expense of snuffing out—or letting outside influences snuff out—that ember of childlike bliss that made life worthwhile. Sure, kudos to the man for overcoming all he had since his life-changing event. Courage, fortitude—he had them in spades. Still. Coping wasn't the same as living. Far from it. And maybe, just maybe, she could stoke that ember.

You don't know that,

Very true. But she didn't know that she couldn't, either. And she wouldn't know unless she tried.

Chapter Six

Leaning against the inn's kitchen counter, his daughter sacked out against his chest, Patrick said to his mother, "So what were you two talking about?"

Chuckling, she glanced over at him as she dried the turkey platter prior to lugging it back home. It'd driven him nuts, not being able to pin her down until now. But there was no way to have a private conversation with two dozen people around.

"This and that," Ma said, setting the platter on the counter before slipping into her coat. "Girl talk, mostly."

"Meaning you're not going to tell me."

"Nope."

She checked the clean kitchen one last time, then excused herself to visit the restroom. His dad wandered in, chewing on a toothpick as he gave the space an approving once-over.

"I wouldn't've thought it possible, what those gals did

with the place." He climbed onto a stool behind the massive island, smiling for Lili. "Brings back memories, how you kids used to pass out like that. Sometimes I miss it." He paused. "You hear from her mother today?"

"No. Not that I expected to."

"Shame. For her sake," Pop said. "Although for yours I can't say I'm sorry Natalie's not in the picture anymore."

Patrick frowned. "You never said that before."

"Didn't feel it was my place."

"And now it is?"

His father was quiet for a long moment, chewing the toothpick. Then he said around it, "She's something else, huh?"

"Who?"

"April, who else? And you know what I think?" He tossed the toothpick in the trash bag waiting to be hauled to the mini Dumpster outside. "I think you should ask her out."

Shifting Lili in his arms, Patrick sighed. "And you've been talking to Luke."

"Maybe. Oh, c'mon—what's the worst that could happen? She says no. No harm, no foul, right? But you gotta start somewhere, put yourself out there."

"And why do we keep having the same conversation?" Patrick whispered, cupping Lili's head when she stirred in her sleep. "I did try putting myself out there, remember? It didn't work."

"So you try again," Dad said, with a slight bow in his direction. "And don't give me that look. You know yourself you've never been a quitter. Right? And anyway, something tells me—" he lowered his voice "—you got a shot with that one, okay?" He grinned. "And you know it, too, don't you?"

"And you're butting in."

Joe shrugged, unconcerned. "Gives me something to live for. Look, all we want is to see you happy again. Like you used to be...uh..."

"Before. Got it."

"It's up to you, son, that's all I'm saying. You've got a lot more control over things than you might want to believe."

"You're right. I do. And the one thing I can control, or at least try to, is how my actions affect Lilianna. She's basically already lost one mother. No way am I putting her through that again."

"So you're gonna live like a monk until she leaves for college?"

"Joe, for heaven's sake," his mother said, returning to dig in her purse for a tube of hand cream. "Leave the boy alone. You want us to take the baby?" she said, squirting the goop into her palm then briskly rubbing her hands together.

Suddenly the thought of letting Lili go was like a stab to the chest. "No," he said, nuzzling her temple. "I'm going straight home. Soon as I talk to April, catch her up on where we stand. *With the grounds,*" he said at his parents' simultaneously lifted brows and faint smiles. "So you two go on, I'll talk to you later."

After a kiss and hug from his mother, a slap on the shoulder from his dad, they left. Took a few minutes to find April, though, in the huge house. But he finally did, in a small den off the gathering room that was part of her private suite. She was curled up on a love seat, wrapped in a throw and staring into the flames in the gas fireplace. At his knock on the door frame, she jumped, then turned that demon-defying smile on him. Those soft sea-colored eyes. And at that moment he knew the worst that could happen, should he do what everyone kept telling him to do, wasn't that she'd say no.

The worst that could happen was that she'd say yes.

* * *

She hadn't meant to eavesdrop, of course. And as it was, she'd hied her little booty away the moment she realized Patrick and his father were talking about her. But she'd heard enough. Enough to realize that Patrick and she had reached some sort of tipping point or whatever you wanted to call it, where they needed to face this thing head-on and make a conscious decision that nothing was ever going to happen or to give it a shot.

Oh, she'd have to take the lead, that much was obvious. Even though that went against every ounce of Good Southern Girl training she'd ever had. But sometimes, a girl just had to channel her inner brazen hussy.

"Hey," she said softly as the hussy checked her makeup, spritzed on some more Aqua Net. "I thought you'd gone."

"Almost," Patrick said. After a long, assessing look that made her toes curl. Or the hussy's. Somebody's. "But we never really had a chance to talk about the damage."

"Oh. Right."

More assessing. More curling. "Although it's not as bad as it looked, thankfully."

"You don't have to stand there, you know. Come on in. Sit."

He did, sitting on the very edge of the wing chair across from her, cradling the tiny girl on his lap so she molded to him. April smiled, trying to ignore the squeeze to her insides. Wasn't working. "Somebody's plumb worn out."

Then he smiled down at his daughter and the squeezing became almost painful. "I think we all are." He glanced around at the room, done up in muted jewel tones. "I hadn't seen this room before. It's nice."

"Yeah, since we cleaned out an entire Dumpster's worth of worthless junk my grandmother had accumulated over the last ten years. But I like that it's cozy. The gathering room feels overwhelming when it's only me."

"I can imagine." A slight frown marred his brow before his gaze fell back to his daughter, a bundle of limp adorableness in a bright green hoodie and purple tutu. The thought of all that fluff in Patrick's big, rough hands made April smile. Finally he looked up, the picture of concern. "Are you okay? I mean, all by yourself in this big place?"

"Oh, sure. Although I'll admit it was a little creepy at first." Was it okay to admit she'd never lived on her own before her marriage? That she'd moved into an apartment after Helene's death because she didn't feel like their house was really hers? "I can't wait for my first guests. And I think I'm going to look for some kind of live-in caretaker. Maybe a couple. Haven't decided yet."

"Sounds like a plan. So anyway…" His gaze slipped slightly to her left. "We saved most of the plantings for now. We can come back on Monday to rebuild the gazebo, replant the few things that are too far gone. It's covered," he said with a slight grin. "Remember? Because you didn't haggle?"

"I see." She fingered the arm of the sofa. Thought she'd take a stab at teasing. "So you did overcharge me."

He actually laughed, loudly enough to make Lili stir. "No. But stuff happens. At least this time we don't have to eat the loss."

"Dear Lord. Does that happen often?"

"What? Oh. No. Not really. We always charge enough to cover our bu…uh, ourselves. When plants die, things like that—"

Do it, the hussy said, huffily. *Do it, do it, do it, do it, do it.*

"Ask me," April said softly, electricity jolting through her. Her cousins would be so proud. Of course, she hadn't asked *him,* to which the hussy was rolling her eyes. But at least she'd given him the opening, right? Baby steps.

Patrick's eyes jerked to hers. "What?"

"Ask me out."

"April—"

"Nothing fancy," she said, hoping she didn't sound desperate. Because she wasn't. Really. "Dinner at Emerson's. Maybe a movie. If things work out…" Her heart thumped against her sternum. "Maybe a good-night kiss at the end."

Oh, dear. He actually flinched. And not, she didn't think, because he found the idea appalling. Frowning though he was. Strange, and wonderful, the feeling of power that gave her.

"I thought I made it clear—"

"What's clear," she said, "is that there's something humming between us. Agreed?"

After a long pause, he nodded. "Agreed." Oh. Wow. Okay, then. Except then he said, "That doesn't mean I feel right about acting on it."

Well, shoot. "Why not?"

"Because I'm not in the market for a relationship, for one thing. And don't know whether I ever will be. You, on the other hand—"

"—see somebody I'd like to get to know better. What's so hard to understand—?"

"Why you'd pick me."

Although his gaze held steady in hers, that wasn't enough to distract her from the distrust she saw there. The disbelief. She half wanted to clobber him upside the head with one of Mel's copper-clad skillets. "Seriously? You're questioning my judgment?"

"More like…your motives."

"I don't pity you, if that's what you mean. And if that *is* what you mean I've half a mind to take the offer off the table." When he pressed his lips together, she heard herself say, even as her heart was pounding to beat the band. "I know what happened. Your mother told me."

On a sigh, Patrick shut his eyes. Opened them again. "She shouldn't've done that."

"Well, she did. So deal." When he glanced away, she said, "Are you *afraid* to ask me out?"

His laugh was rough. "No. Just using common sense."

Which she took to mean the same thing. Honestly, the man was just asking for that skillet.

"Well I am," she said. "And I don't care who knows it."

"Oh, yeah?" He almost smiled. "Could've fooled me."

"I've had a lot of practice sounding braver than I am." Even if not a lot of practice at…other things. Although something told her— That mouth. Oh, my—she'd be a quick study. "But inside? A bundle of nerves."

He seemed to consider this for a moment, then said, "That why you didn't ask *me* out?"

"No, I didn't ask you because, for one thing, I'm an old-fashioned girl—" that got a snigger "—and for another, *you* need to do this."

"That so?"

"Yeah." April stood, tugging down over her hips the sweater she'd changed into for dinner. "But you know what? You're right. If you don't think you're ready, or that our going out would be a waste of your time or energy, or whatever excuse you're buying into, then I'm done. Because arguing with a brick wall is a waste of *my* time and energy—"

He practically surged to his feet, shifting Lili in his arms so her head flopped onto his shoulder, her mouth sagging open—oh, Lord, death by cute—and April braced herself for the explosion. Or the Dramatic Exit. His laugh, though—she hadn't expected that.

"Tomorrow night. Seven. I'll pick you up. Lock the door behind me."

And off he strode, God-only-knew-what going through his head and leaving April far too wobbly kneed to move. Finally she did, though, holding on to things as she made her way to the door to flip the dead bolt. Then she slid to the floor, palm flattened against her chest, as the word "ramifications" exploded in her brain.

"You're kidding?" April's eyes glinted mischievously at Patrick from across the white-clothed table in the quiet little restaurant in Salisbury. Although they'd agreed to keep things casual, she'd put up her hair, was sporting a little more makeup than he remembered her wearing before. Just enough to make her mouth look softer, her eyes even bigger. "Your family really doesn't know we're doing this?"

"You've met my family," he said, tilting his beer glass to his lips. "Would you tell them?"

"Good point."

Obviously nothing would come of this, he thought over the pinch of guilt. But sometimes it was easier to play along until the other party realized pursuing a dumb idea doesn't make it less dumb. So he'd been a little taken aback, frankly, at how easily they'd chatted on the ride here, thanks to April peppering him with questions about his family. About Lili. Stuff he could talk about without thinking too hard.

Of course, nobody'd told him to bring her here, to a place with tablecloths and candlelight and picture-free menus written in some fancy print. He could've taken her to Emerson's, like she'd suggested. Could've honked for her in front of the inn, let her climb up into the truck on her own instead of going around and helping her in. Could've responded to her questions with monosyllabic grunts. He wasn't a prick, but still. There were all sorts of ways to put a woman off the scent.

Speaking of scents, her perfume...

Damn.

April messed with her fork, made a fist, tucked both hands underneath the table. "So who's taking care of Lilianna?"

"Grad student who lives downstairs from us. She and Lili are nuts about each other." Although Lili had still pouted when he'd left, her lower lip quivering when he'd given her a wave as he walked out the door.

"Not to worry," April said, "my cousins don't know, either." She took a tiny sip of her white wine, eyeing the glass when she set it back down like she didn't quite trust it.

"The wine okay?"

"Um, sure. I guess." A smile flickered. "I don't really drink much, as a rule."

"Not even in college?"

"Never went to college. No time. Or money." She shrugged. "I worked all the way through high school as well. Had to."

There she went again, stating a fact but somehow without playing the sympathy card. Just letting him know that things hadn't been that great, no biggie. Then she reached up to tug loose a strand of hair slightly tangled in the drapey neck of her soft blue sweater, twisting it around her finger for a moment before catching herself, like she had with the fork earlier. It was both weirdly appealing and damned unsettling, how she'd seesaw between being bodacious one minute and like a kitten exploring the big wide world for the first time the next. And, no, that was not protectiveness surging in his gut—

"Hey."

Her gaze touched his.

"You nervous?"

"Heck, yeah," she said on a little laugh. "It's been…" Her lips scrunched together as she reached for the fork again, carefully lining it up with the edge of her napkin. "I never really dated much." One side of her mouth canted. "Either."

"Before your husband, you mean?"

"No. Ever."

"Here you go," the cheerful, tattooed waitress said, setting a shrimp cocktail in front of April, oysters on the half shell for him. "Need anything else, hon?"

"No, thanks," Patrick said, almost abruptly, leaning toward April as soon as she left. "You and your husband never dated?"

Fine, so sue him—he was curious. Or maybe it was the perfume fumes.

She shook her head, not looking at him as she stabbed her first shrimp. Over and over. "Clayton and I…" She cleared her throat, then pushed out another breathy laugh before finally dispatching the poor mangled shrimp. "And this is where you can tell I'm real inexperienced at this, since I have no idea what's considered proper first-date conversation."

And feeling bad for her was not part of the plan. At all. No, the plan was that he'd be polite, sure, but boring. Attentive, but not too attentive. "How about we make up our own rules? Say whatever we feel needs saying."

"Works for me." She shoved another shrimp into her mouth, licking off a smear of sauce on her lower lip. "Long as you don't leave me stranded."

"Nah," Patrick said after a moment. "I'll make sure to call your cousin after I've disappeared to the men's room."

She laughed then, and it made him feel good.

So good it made him mad, which he supposed didn't make a whole lot of sense.

Then again, life in general didn't make a whole lot of sense.

"So. Clayton and I—"

The crash made him yell, duck, bolt to his feet in the space of a second, his heart about to tear through his chest. Dizzy, disoriented, he gripped the top of the booth, his fragmented brain desperately trying to kick in, make a decision.

"Patrick!"

His heart still throbbing, he whipped around, grabbed April's arm. "You okay?"

Confusion flittered across her features before she smiled. "I'm fine," she said softly, rubbing his upper arm with her free hand. "And so are you. Somebody dropped some dishes in the kitchen. That's all."

With a violent shudder, he returned to the here and now enough to feel the sweat between his shoulder blades, the oysters threatening to rebel in his stomach. Swallowing hard, he slid back into the booth. "Everybody's looking at me—"

"Tough," she said, sitting back down, as well, and way, *way* in the back of his brain, he wanted to laugh. Hell, he was shaking so bad he must look like he had the DTs. He rubbed a trembling hand over his face, then grabbed his water glass, got it to his mouth, gulped half of it down.

"Dishes," he repeated stupidly.

"Yep. Dishes. My guess is somebody's backside is in a major sling right now. Hey…look at me." When he finally met that calm, steady gaze, she said, very quietly, "You wanna stay or go?"

"I…I don't know. Go, I think. I'm sorry…"

"Hush," she said, signaling to the waitress. "These things happen. And you put that away—"

"I am *not* letting you pay," he said, grateful to see his hand had more or less stopped shaking when he dug his credit card out of his wallet. That his signature was clear enough—as clear as it ever was, anyway, he had the world's worst handwriting—when he signed the slip a few minutes later. And he was especially thankful when they walked outside, to feel the damp, chilly breeze slap what was left of the attack to kingdom come.

"You okay to drive?" she asked when they reached his truck in the parking lot. "Or do you want me to?"

"No, I'm fine."

"You sure?"

"Yes! Dammit, April! I'm fine, okay!" Except he wasn't, was he? And in all likelihood, never would be. Not completely. Frustrated, furious, he wheeled on her. "Or are you afraid I'm gonna lose it if I pop a tire, or a car backfires behind us? Get us both killed?"

Again with the fearless gaze. "How often does it happen?" she asked, so gently it hurt.

Patrick propped a wrist on the truck's roof, ignoring the Siren call of the cigarettes he'd quit two years before. "Not like it used to. When I first…got out." Granted, it'd been months, more than a year, actually, since he'd had an episode, but he sure wasn't "cured," was he? "Still an issue, though." His mouth pulled into a tight, humorless smile. "Obviously."

"So let me ask you this—do you worry when you have Lili with you?"

Fear iced his spine. "I force myself not to think about it."

Shivering, April stuffed her hands in the pockets of her long coat. "Then either force yourself not to think about it now, or let me drive. Your call. But make up your mind because in case you hadn't noticed, it's freezing out here."

He helped her into the truck, then stamped around to his side and got in. With a surreptitious check to make sure his hands were steady before ramming the key into the ignition, he backed out.

Yeah, he'd wanted her to see this was headed nowhere. But not like this.

Damn it, not like this.

Not surprisingly, nobody said much for some time after they started back to the inn. Even though April was grateful that Patrick's anger and embarrassment had both dissipated by the time they got in the truck, she doubted he was in the mood for idle chatter.

And she certainly didn't think this was the time to resume their interrupted conversation about her marriage. Not that she'd intended to blurt out everything, especially since her cousins both seemed convinced the V-word tended to make men break out in hives. And/or run like hell. Something about not being able to handle the pressure.

It all seemed very silly to April. Because what was the big hairy deal? Really. For pity's sake, she read. She knew things. You either were, or you weren't. Big whoop. Although she did have to agree it probably wasn't the smartest thing to bring up on a first date.

Or, in this case, probably their only date.

As it was, she'd already strongly suspected Patrick had only cowed to the pressure to ask her out in order to get everyone—including her—off his back. So, you know, the next time some family member or other brought up the subject, he could say, "Actually, we did go out, it didn't take, so can we move on?" Oh, he'd been perfectly lovely all evening. Prior to his freak-out, that is. But perhaps a trifle *too* lovely for someone who'd given her a pretty good glimpse of the beast he kept chained inside him.

Now she knew why he kept the chains on. Or tried to, at least.

She stole a glance at that rock-solid jaw as he drove, the ravaged skin looking far worse in the truck's shadowy interior. When she'd teased him that he smelled better than she did, he'd sheepishly admitted it was the moisturizer he had to use every day. That he'd found out the hard way there was no such thing as completely unscented. Poor guy. And wouldn't he have a cow if he could read her mind right now? But he was clearly doing everything in his power to gain dominion over this, this *thing* constantly lurking in his thoughts, his experience, determined to gobble up all the progress he'd made.

"Sorry," Patrick said, startling her. "Guess I'm not used to having somebody ride with me who actually expects me to talk."

"It's okay, I was kind of lost in thought myself."

"About?"

"You."

His hand flexed on the wheel. "Not sure that's worth using up brain cells for."

"You want me to smack you with this bag, or what? And you might want to think carefully how you answer. I don't travel light."

She thought he almost smiled. "And *you* might want to have that violent streak checked out before you do any real damage."

April laughed. "As if. Although there was this time, when my cousins and I were kids…" She paused, grinning, reliving the incident like it'd happened yesterday, feeling the sun beat on her mostly bare back, her nostrils tingling with the tang of Banana Boat sunscreen…

"We were always smacking at each other—we still do—although just goofing around, you know? Nobody ever got hurt. But one day we were sunbathing out on the dock behind the house, and I think Blythe was all hormonal or whatever and Mel said something she took issue with. I don't even remember how I got dragged into it, but suddenly we were all three going at each other like chickens in a barnyard, completely forgetting how close we were to the edge of the dock. Blythe was bigger than Mel and me, of course, and she swung at Mel, who stumbled into me and grabbed Blythe…and over we all went into the water. Good times."

Finally Patrick laughed. "You gals are close, I take it?"

"We are, yeah. Like sisters more than cousins, since we're all only children. Got up each other's noses like sisters, too. But we were only together during the summers. And even that ended by the time we were in high school."

"So you lost touch?"

"We did. Isn't that strange? Or maybe not—Blythe went on to college, of course, and Mel had a baby. Quinn. You met her at dinner the other night."

"Right. Wait—is…that why they moved away? Mel and her mother?"

"Apparently so. And given our family's propensity for keeping secrets from each other…" She shrugged. "Still. Until the house brought us back together, I hadn't realized how much I'd missed them."

"I can imagine."

They passed at least three highway markers before April worked up the nerve to ask him, "Your family…I assume they've been a huge help with your recovery?"

"Yeah," he said after a moment. "Not that they don't drive me crazy, too, more often than not, but I know I wouldn't have made it through without them."

"And have you, um, had other kinds of help? Therapies? Procedures…?"

Silence.

"I'm sorry," April said, "you don't have to answer that."

"Meds, for a while. But it seemed like cheating, somehow. Numbing things instead of dealing with them. For me, anyway. For other people they seem to work okay. Anyway, so I ditched those, did talk therapy instead. About talked my brains out, too." He paused. "I am getting better. Like you said, my family, working—being with Lili—it all helps."

"I'm sure it does."

After another pause, he said, "Scaring you wasn't part of the game plan."

"Tonight, you mean?"

"Point to you," he muttered, then pushed out a breath. "But back there…I couldn't control that."

"I understand," she said softly, knowing better than to mention the fear in his voice. "I wasn't, though. Scared. That time or this. Concerned, sure. But not for myself. For you." She paused. "I don't spook easily."

"Really."

"Yeah. Really."

"This from the woman who was nervous as hell about the date."

When her eyes cut to his profile this time, she caught the smile. Not a full-out one, perhaps, but enough to make her feel that maybe things had eased inside his head. About them. "Nervous is not the same as spooked. Lots of things make me nervous, but usually about my own abilities. If I'm gonna make the grade at something. Like if the inn will be a success. That, I worry about constantly. But very little actually frightens me."

He chuckled. "Except my face."

She slumped down in her seat. "That was shock. Not fright."

Another soft laugh preceded, "Anybody ever tell you you're nuts?"

"My mother." April sighed out. "Every chance she gets. Especially about me and the inn. She's not exactly on board."

"Then *she's* nuts. Sorry," he said when April laughed. "But it's true. Because even from what little I've observed, you strike me as…as somebody who knows the meaning of determination. I don't doubt for a minute you'll make a go of this, April. Not for one single minute."

Bowled over by his unexpected support, April faced forward, blinking for a couple of seconds before saying, "Thanks."

"No problem," he said, sounding a little floored himself.

Moving on, she thought, then said, "And don't look now, but you're not doing a half-bad job at keeping up a conversation. And anyway, what about Lili? Don't you guys chat when you're together?"

He snorted. "Lili does enough talking for both of us. All I have to do is say, 'Uh-huh,' every so often. That's the thing about a four-year-old, it doesn't take much to make them happy."

And there it was again, the melancholy he hung on to like a worn-out T-shirt, all misshapen and full of holes. Useless.

"You're a good dad," she said.

A moment passed. "You don't know me well enough to say that."

"Says the man convinced I'll make a success of the inn."

He shifted, as though loading up for another protest, then sighed. "I do my best. Whether that's enough or not, I don't know."

"You love her. That's enough."

"Is it?" he said quietly, focused on the road. "Is love by itself enough?"

Oh, *Lord,* the man was pitiful. *Pitiful.* Yes, she understood there were mitigating circumstances, that some people might say he had every right to feel sorry for himself. But his family sure as heck didn't, so neither would she.

"Guess that depends on the people involved," she murmured.

"Exactly." He glanced over at her, then back out the windshield. And practically growled, "Depends on the people involved."

So much for prodding him out of his funk.

They pulled into the inn's driveway as a piddly snow began to dot the windshield. Patrick sighed. "This was sure one lousy date, wasn't it?"

"It was different, I'll grant you that, but lousy—"

"For God's sake, April!" The truck crunched to a stop; Patrick cut the ignition and slapped one arm across the old-school bench seat, his gaze drilling into hers. "Why can't you be like every other woman? I crapped out on you before we even got the main course, or you had a chance to tell me whatever you were going to tell me—yes, I remembered—then I don't talk to you for most of the ride home, and you act like, like…like none of it bothers you in the least!"

"Well, it doesn't!" she shot back. "Except now that you mention it, I am starving."

He stared at her for a moment, then looked back out the windshield, shaking his head. "That doesn't even make sense."

"That I'm starving?"

He sighed. "No."

Not sure where this was going, April snagged her purse

YOUR PARTICIPATION IS REQUESTED!

Dear Reader,

Since you are a lover of romance fiction – we would like to get to know you!

Inside you will find a short Reader's Survey. Sharing your answers with us will help our editorial staff understand who you are and what activities you enjoy.

To thank you for your participation, we would like to send you 2 books and 2 gifts – **ABSOLUTELY FREE!**

Enjoy your gifts with our appreciation,

Pam Powers

**SEE INSIDE
FOR READER'S
SURVEY**

For Your Romance Reading Pleasure...

We'll send you 2 books and 2 gifts
ABSOLUTELY FREE
just for completing our Reader's Survey!

YOURS FREE! We'll send you
two fabulous surprise gifts absolutely FREE,
just for trying our Romance books!

Visit us at:
www.ReaderService.com

YOUR READER'S SURVEY
"THANK YOU" FREE GIFTS INCLUDE:
- ▶ 2 Harlequin® Special Edition books
- ▶ 2 lovely surprise gifts

▶ DETACH AND MAIL CARD TODAY! ▶

PLEASE FILL IN THE CIRCLES COMPLETELY TO RESPOND

1) What type of fiction books do you enjoy reading? (Check all that apply)
- ○ Suspense/Thrillers ○ Action/Adventure ○ Modern-day Romances
- ○ Historical Romance ○ Humour ○ Paranormal Romance

2) What attracted you most to the last fiction book you purchased on impulse?
- ○ The Title ○ The Cover ○ The Author ○ The Story

3) What is usually the greatest influencer when you <u>plan</u> to buy a book?
- ○ Advertising ○ Referral ○ Book Review

4) How often do you access the internet?
- ○ Daily ○ Weekly ○ Monthly ○ Rarely or never.

5) How many NEW paperback fiction novels have you purchased in the past 3 months?
- ○ 0 - 2 ○ 3 - 6 ○ 7 or more

YES! I have completed the Reader's Survey. Please send me the 2 FREE books and 2 FREE gifts (gifts are worth about $10) for which I qualify. I understand that I am under no obligation to purchase any books, as explained on the back of this card.

235/335 HDL FNPJ

FIRST NAME	LAST NAME

ADDRESS

APT.#	CITY

STATE/PROV.   ZIP/POSTAL CODE

Offer limited to one per household and not applicable to series that subscriber is currently receiving.
Your Privacy – The Reader Service is committed to protecting your privacy. Our Privacy Policy is available online at www.ReaderService.com or upon request from the Reader Service. We make a portion of our mailing list available to reputable third parties that offer products we believe may interest you. If you prefer that we not exchange your name with third parties, or if you wish to clarify or modify your communication preferences, please visit us at www.ReaderService.com/consumerschoice or write to us at Reader Service Preference Service, P.O. Box 9062, Buffalo, NY 14269. Include your complete name and address.

© 2012 HARLEQUIN ENTERPRISES LIMITED
® and ™ are trademarks owned and used by the trademark owner and/or its licensee. Printed in the U.S.A.

The Reader Service — Here's How It Works:

Accepting your 2 free books and 2 free gifts (gifts valued at approximately $10.00) places you under no obligation to buy anything. You may keep the books and gifts and return the shipping statement marked "cancel." If you do not cancel, about a month later we'll send you 6 additional books and bill you just $4.49 each in the U.S. or $5.24 each in Canada. That is a savings of at least 14% off the cover price. It's quite a bargain! Shipping and handling is just 50¢ per book in the U.S. and 75¢ per book in Canada.* You may cancel at any time, but if you choose to continue, every month we'll send you 6 more books, which you may either purchase at the discount price or return to us and cancel your subscription.

*Terms and prices subject to change without notice. Prices do not include applicable taxes. Sales tax applicable in N.Y. Canadian residents will be charged applicable taxes. Offer not valid in Quebec. Books received may not be as shown. All orders subject to credit approval. Credit or debit balances in a customer's account(s) may be offset by any other outstanding balance owed by or to the customer. Please allow 4 to 6 weeks for delivery. Offer available while quantities last.

If offer card is missing write to: The Reader Service, P.O. Box 1867, Buffalo, NY 14240-1867 or visit: www.ReaderService.com

BUSINESS REPLY MAIL
FIRST-CLASS MAIL   PERMIT NO. 717   BUFFALO, NY

POSTAGE WILL BE PAID BY ADDRESSEE

THE READER SERVICE
PO BOX 1341
BUFFALO NY 14240-8571

NO POSTAGE
NECESSARY
IF MAILED
IN THE
UNITED STATES

off the truck floor, hugging it to her middle. "Would you rather I be whiny and pouty?"

"Yes, dammit!"

Biting her lip, she faced him again. "And you think *I'm* not making sense?"

"What I actually said was, that *this* doesn't make sense."

She cocked her head, frowning. "This?"

His gaze once again met hers. And held.

Oh. *This*. Got it.

Except…she didn't.

Then he reached over to palm her jaw, making her breath catch and her heart trip an instant before he kissed her. Kissed her good. Oh, *so* good, his tongue teasing hers in a way that made everything snap into focus and melt at the same time—

Then he backed away, hand still on jaw, eyes still boring into hers. Tortured, what-the-*heck*-am-I-doing? eyes. "If things had gone like I planned, this would've been where I dropped you off, said something about, yeah, I had a nice time, too, I'll call you, and driven away with no intention whatsoever of calling you."

"With or without the kiss?"

"*That* kiss? Without."

O-kaay. "Noted. Except…you wouldn't do that."

His brow knotted. "Do what?"

"Tell me you'll call if you're not going to. Because that is not how you roll, Patrick Shaughnessy."

He let go to drop his head against the headrest, emitting a short, rough laugh. "You're going to be the death of me."

"Not intentionally," she said, and he laughed again. But it was such a sad laugh, tears sprang to April's eyes.

"No, tonight did not go as planned," he said. "In any way, shape, form or fashion. But weirdly enough in some ways it went better." Another humorless laugh. "Or would have, if you'd been a normal woman."

"As in, whiny and pouty."

"As in, not somebody who'd still be sitting here after what happened. Who would've been out of this truck before I'd even put it in Park. But here you are…" In the dim light, she saw his eyes glisten a moment before he turned, slamming his hand against the steering wheel.

"I don't *want* this, April! Don't want…you inside my head, seeing how messy it is in there! Don't want…"

He stopped, breathing hard, and April could practically hear him think, *Don't want my heart broken again.*

She turned, fidgeting with her purse strap, considering the wisdom of taking his words to heart. Of saying, "Okay, if that's what you really want…" and getting out of the truck, walking back to that empty old house and never pestering the man again. That would be the smart thing, all right. And heaven knew it would be the easy thing.

But that didn't mean it would be the right thing.

Especially when she remembered what his mother had said, about his needing comfort whether he thought he did or not. And also, it was about this little voice—heck, a big, booming voice—telling her they needed each other.

She took a deep, steadying breath and said, "So does this mean you're going to call, or not?"

Silence. Then a groan. April looked over, right as he dragged his gaze to hers. "Does that mean the evening's over?"

Her heart did a somersault. "Don't you have to get back to Lili?"

The corners of his mouth curved. A teensy bit. "Not until eleven."

"Well, then," April said, plopping her purse back down by her feet. "I don't know about you, but I'd *kill* for a hamburger. And then, if it's all the same to you? I wouldn't mind a few more of those kisses." She slid her eyes to his. "If you're amenable, of course."

After a moment, Patrick started to laugh. A big, full-bellied laugh the likes of which she'd never heard out of his mouth before.

"Oh, I'm amenable," he said, finally, shifting back into Drive and pulling back onto the road, and she thought, *Hang on tight, honey.*

And she wasn't talking about his driving skills.

Chapter Seven

Round Two, Patrick thought twenty minutes later, after they'd loaded up on burgers and fries and shakes at some fast food joint out on the highway and were headed back to her place, the truck's cab filled with the scent of frying oil and April's perfume. Apparently she really was starving, stuffing fries in her mouth at an alarming rate as she bopped along to something their parents might've listened to in 1974.

"There are other stations, you know."

"No, I like this," she said, scrunching down in her seat as much as the seat belt would let her and propping her feet—in little black flat shoes that were strangely sexy— on the dashboard. The snow was too half-assed to be of any real concern, the soft flakes lazily slithering down the windshield. "Makes me feel like a little kid again—oh, I love this part!"

Waving a fry for emphasis, she belted out the refrain. Yep, nuts, all right.

She held out the bag of fries, shaking it until he took one. Not that he was particularly hungry, his stomach still knotted from both the attack and that kiss.

Oh, man…that kiss. Talk about not making any sense. And he sure as hell hadn't seen it coming, any more than April probably had. Hadn't been any real thought behind it, just…instinct. And a purely selfish instinct, at that, some primal need to connect, to make everything stop spinning, to feel like a normal human being again.

By rights she should've been appalled. Or at least put off. But no. Oh, no, she'd…she'd melted into the kiss like she'd been waiting for it all her life. Kissed him back, too. Kissed him back good.

And then asked for more.

Kee-rap.

She crumpled the empty fries box and stuffed it back into the bag, then sucked loudly on her milkshake straw. Exactly like a little kid. Despite himself, Patrick chuckled. In another life, another world, he could fall for this little nutjob. Fall real hard. But he wouldn't. Couldn't.

"You act like you never had one of those before."

She laughed. "I don't very often. But when I do, I make it my business to thoroughly enjoy it. Maybe because when I was a kid, fast food was a special treat."

"Because your parents wouldn't let you have it?"

"No, because we could rarely afford it. True, my arteries will thank me some day, but…"

"But what?"

"Nothing," she said, squeaking her straw in and out of the shake's lid.

"And nothing grinds my gears worse than when somebody doesn't finish their sentence. Unless it's that godawful sound you're making with the straw."

"Sorry," she said, setting her cup in the holder in her

door before folding her arms across her stomach. "It's like I have a split personality or something. Not in a psychotic way, I don't mean that. But there's part of me—a big part—that has a real problem with keeping secrets. Unfortunately there's a lot of stuff in my past that either makes people uncomfortable or makes them feel sorry for me. Only if I don't feel particularly sorry for myself, I don't see why anybody else should feel that way." Her eyes cut to his. "You know what I mean, right?"

"I do. So?"

"So…I had kind of an unusual childhood. Although of course I didn't realize it was unusual until I was a teenager. See, my father was—still is, I suppose—a dreamer. Always had these big ideas, big ideas that would liberate him from working for The Man—although he rarely worked for The Man in the first place," she said with a grimace. "And my mother, bless her heart, she bought into his dreams. Every single time. She was a teacher, so we could've gotten by on her salary—if barely—if it hadn't been for all of Daddy's 'investments.'"

"And she never put her foot down?"

"Oh, she made noises about it, had periodic conniptions. And then my dad would promise to find a 'real' job—which he would, for a few months, a year—until he'd come up with another idea, and the cycle would start all over again."

"Is he…are your parents still together?"

"As in, joined at the hip." She paused. "Dad was real sick, though, a few years back. He's much better now, but that seemed to put the kibosh on his ambitions." Her mouth twisted. "For now, at least. But long story short, I know what 'poor' is. And I know I like where I am now a lot better."

"Which I suppose is why you don't feel sorry for yourself."

"Because I'm no longer indigent? No." She picked up her shake again, took another pull on the straw. "Not that I'm not being smart about my money—although it still feels weird to call it 'my' money—but that's not where my trust is. No, my confidence, I guess you can call it, comes from knowing I'll always have choices." A van pulled up behind them, passed on the left, the snow sparkling in the red glow from its taillights as it zoomed ahead. "That I'm a lot more in charge of my own destiny than I might've thought when I was a kid."

"You really believe that?"

Her laughter warmed him. "I don't mean I think I can control the future. But I can control what I do about it. To some extent, at least. When I'm presented with options, it's up to me and nobody else to choose which one of those is best for me. And if that choice doesn't work out…" She shrugged. "There's always something else waiting in the wings. Even if I can't see it right then."

The snowfall thickened; Patrick tightened his grip on the wheel. "Huh."

April laughed. "Didn't mean to get so heavy on you, but…yeah. That's kind of how I felt, too, when it first hit me. Huh. That I didn't have to lie down and take whatever fate decided to dish out."

"Like your mother did, you mean?"

"But, see, since Mama was the one earning a living— she held the power. So she could've left my father anytime she wanted. She *chose* to stay."

"Why?"

"Because she loved him? Because she preferred a man who at least *had* dreams, as opposed to one willing to simply settle for the status quo? Who knows? But in any case, that was her choice." April fiddled with her seat belt. "I don't know that it would've been mine. In her shoes, I mean."

Patrick mulled over all that for a few seconds, then said, "So what you're saying is, you don't buy into the notion that we're trapped by circumstances."

"Only as much as we believe we are. I mean, look how far you've come."

"And here we are," he said, pulling up in front of the house. "Again."

"Oh. Wow. Already. Um...you want to come inside?"

"The snow's getting heavier, I should probably be getting back."

"I suppose you're right." April gathered up her purse, the shake, the bag with her hamburger. "But..."

Patrick sighed. "I suppose you're still wanting another kiss."

"If it's not an imposition."

He could hear the smile in her voice. The teasing. The implication, that wanting him to kiss her again was her choice. That, for whatever reason, she'd chosen him. This sweet, funny, gorgeous gal had chosen *him*.

Now if only he could figure out what to make of that.

At the moment, though, he owed her a kiss. So, since her lap was full, he leaned over to cup her jaw, lower his mouth to hers, a mouth that was cool and tasted of chocolate and French fries...a mouth that instantly warmed when she opened to him, inviting him to explore.

Need shot straight to his groin, even as another kind of need—to protect her, from him, from herself—swelled inside his chest to where he could barely breathe.

His breathing unsteady, he pulled back, feeling like he'd shut Pandora's box in the nick of time...only she grabbed the front of his jacket with her one free hand and yanked him close, laughing, and he caught the impish glint in her eyes a moment before their mouths met again.

…and the box flew open, setting free everything he'd kept locked up for far too long, everything he refused to let himself think about, things like passion and closeness and connection, the simple pleasure of being with someone who wanted to be with him.

This time, April broke the kiss, her hand pressed to his chest where she could obviously feel his jackhammering heart. "Go home to your little girl," she whispered, then leaned forward one last time to place a gentle kiss on his scarred cheek before grinning into his eyes. "I'm not going anywhere."

He waited, both to make sure she was safe inside the house and for his body to readjust to pre-kiss levels before carefully steering the truck back onto the road.

I'm not going anywhere…

Twenty minutes later, after he'd paid Shelley and gone in to check on Lili, straightening her covers and rearranging her favorite stuffed toys around her, April's words still played over and over in his head. A promise? Or a challenge? Or both?

For several seconds Patrick watched his daughter sleep. Convinced Lili was all he'd ever have, he'd made her his everything. His family, his work—they were important, sure. And he was grateful to both, for helping him regain his sense of purpose. A lot of vets weren't so fortunate. But Lili…

He reached out, stroked a curl off her cheek. She stirred, grabbing her stuffed Piglet before sticking her thumb in her mouth. Everything he'd done so far, had figured on doing for the foreseeable future, was for her. Except she'd go on to live her own life, make her own choices. And while he hoped, prayed, he'd always be a part of it, he wouldn't be the center of it, would he?

And then what?

With a sigh, he tore himself away and headed to the kitchen where he'd dumped the bedraggled bag containing his own burger and fries on the table. His jacket shucked off and tossed across the closest chair, he upended the bag, only to grimace. Nothing more unappetizing that stone-cold fries. Although the burger came in a close second. Clearly he was not meant to get dinner tonight.

Or to find peace, he thought as he stuffed the uneaten food back in the bag and dropped it in the garbage, then walked back to the window in his tiny living room, the street glittering from the fresh dusting of snow. On the plus side, he liked April. A lot. Liked being with her. Liked how she made him laugh, how she refused to put up with his crap. And heaven knew it wouldn't be a hardship to make love to her, a thought that made his breath catch in his chest, that he was even considering something he'd assumed swiped off the table when Natalie left him.

With a woman like April, at least.

But it wouldn't be easy, either. Driving home, he'd finally put the pieces together—that it wasn't a coincidence, was it, that he'd gone on his first date in months and bam! He also had his first attack in nearly that long. And hell, yeah, that scared him, that trying to move forward might actually set him back. How could he justify taking that kind of risk, when Lili's very safety could be at stake?

Sure, April had been a brick tonight, said she wasn't going anywhere. And he had no doubt she meant it. Especially, he thought, with a half laugh, if she was anything like her mother. But what if the attacks did start up again on a regular basis? Could she handle it?

Could he handle seeing the fire go out in her eyes, when she finally and fully realized what she'd gotten herself into?

And yet.

And yet.

It also wasn't a coincidence that whatever progress he'd made—physically, mentally, emotionally—had been *because* he'd taken risks. Pushed himself past the fear, the doubts. What if tonight hadn't been about relapse, but about growing? About being given another shot at living life as fully as he had "before"? Or at least to come pretty damn close. April was giving him a choice, wasn't she?

And whether to take that shot or not was entirely up to him.

He'd called.

A can of soda pressed against her collarbone, April stood at one of the gathering room's bay windows the Monday after Thanksgiving, grinning like some gooney teenager as she watched Patrick and his crew set the grounds to rights again.

He'd *called.*

Granted, the conversation had been short. And blunt, that he was up for taking another step forward, but he couldn't see beyond that. *Could anybody?* she'd thought as she assured him that was okay. That he'd come this far was huge, even if he didn't fully realize it yet.

In any case, he'd said Lili was staying with his sister and her kids tonight so maybe they could get together? Do something?

Her heart pitter-patted as she considered what color underwear should she put on.

Because she had a pretty good idea where the evening would lead, a thought that gave her goose bumps in some very interesting places. Especially when she'd gone out to say hello after he and the crew arrived, and he'd caught her eyes in his and oh, *Lordy,* she'd thought she'd melt on the spot.

You ready for this? the gaze had said, loud and crystal clear, and her girly bits had gone all quivery as they answered back, *You betcha, honey.*

Almost as if they knew what to expect. Or had real high hopes, anyway.

Of course, since Patrick hadn't exactly been subtle with the eat-her-up-with-his-eyes routine, now his whole crew *knew.* Including, unfortunately, his two older brothers. And although she could tell they were pleased for him—if not immensely relieved—she might have liked to keep things under wraps for a moment or two longer—

"Stare at the poor guy any harder," Blythe said beside her, her arms full of fresh pine garland to wrap around the banister, "and he's going to combust. Which would kind of defeat the purpose."

"Where do you want these?" Mel said, carting in a big cardboard box from Blythe's work van.

"Anywhere, they're for the tree. So, spill," Blythe said as Mel deposited the box in the middle of the floor. "Since I notice Ice Man is giving you the same ravenous look you're giving him. Aw, look, Mel…April's blushing!"

"Or running a raging fever. What's going on?"

"Patrick and I…went out. The night after Thanksgiving."

"No!" Mel sank onto a nearby chair. "How did I not know this?"

"Because you were with me," Blythe said, "Black Friday shopping yourself senseless."

"Oh, yeah. Forgot. So…?" Mel gave her an evil grin. "What happened?"

"And maybe that's none of your business," April said,

getting on her knees to paw through the box, pulling out a paper bag of delicate, old-fashioned straw ornaments. "Gosh, Blythe, these are pretty—"

"And you are not hijacking this conversation. This is us, remember? Hey," her oldest cousin said, "I told you about *my* first time. Fair's fair."

"You were fif*teen,* Blythe," April said, continuing to dig, this time unearthing a bunch of whimsical wooden animals. "At that point all you wanted to do was scandalize Mel and me."

"She's got a point, hon," Mel said, and Blythe smacked her with the end of the garland.

April laughed. "And anyway…this wasn't like that."

"Meaning you're still—?"

"Do you think we should put the tree by the window? Or out in the entryway, by the stairs?"

"April!" Hands flailed. Bracelets jangled. "For God's sake!"

She supposed it wasn't entirely fair, within the parameters of their relationship, to remain completely tight-lipped about the evening. Even if, at the time, Blythe had perhaps shared more than she should've, April thought with a smile, remembering how as a thirteen-year-old she'd been equally thrilled and horrified by her cousin's all-too-detailed recounting of her exploits.

Still, as she finally gave them an abbreviated, and somewhat reconstructed, account of the evening—Patrick's panic attack was definitely off-limits—she felt as though she were in a time warp, the conversation sounding a dozen years old, even in her own head. She wasn't a child. Or innocent. Far from it, given her childhood, some of the drudge jobs she'd done, those four years with Clayton and his mother. Except in this one thing…

"So that was it. We came home after the restaurant and then…well…we…"

"Gah, you're killing me, here."

She looked up at Blythe. "Fine. He kissed me."

"Okay, promising. And then…?"

"He kissed me again? Or I kissed him. I don't exactly remember."

"So you made out?"

"Maybe."

Mel and Blythe exchanged glances before Mel laughed. "You guess? You honestly don't know?"

"Does it matter?"

"You are one little weirdo," Blythe muttered, shaking her head. "So did anything else happen? Did he cop a feel? What I mean is, did he—"

"I know what it means, sheesh! But I had a bunch of bags and stuff in my lap. So no." Another exchanged glance. And a double sigh. "They were pretty hot kisses, though. At least, they were hot to me. And when we finished…his eyes were…you know."

"Glassy?"

"Yeah."

Her cousins high-fived each other, although Mel shook her head. "I still can't believe…" She blew out a breath. "You never even got hot and heavy with some guy in high school?"

"Hell, middle school," Blythe said.

"And you don't think I would've told you if I had? Back then, I mean." Because even then, being the youngest had been a pain in the patoot, always feeling like she was playing catch-up.

Horror filled Blythe's eyes. "Please tell me you've at least been kissed."

April laughed. "Yes, I've been kissed," she said, earning her twin sighs of relief from her audience. But *gah,* was right—between Blythe's precocious experimentation with her high school boyfriends and Mel's having Quinn at seventeen, never mind that the circumstances behind that hadn't exactly been ideal, sometimes April wondered how she was even related to these women.

Or to the human race, when it came right down to it.

Even so… "Anyway, this isn't about then. It's about now. And…we're going out again tonight."

And she blushed. Again. Worse than before.

She was still on the carpet by the box. Now both cousins came and sat beside her, Blythe slipping her arm around her shoulders. "And you're worried you'll make a fool of yourself."

"Something like that, yeah. That he'll be disappointed." She pointed to her chest. "These aren't exactly awe inspiring, you know."

Mel chuckled. "Trust me, the only thing he's going to notice is that you have them."

"You got that right," Blythe said, then gave her a squeeze. "You have condoms?"

Blushing again, she nodded. "Bought them yesterday." Several kinds. And sizes. At some convenience store in Easton she could never set foot in again. "And I still think I should, you know. Warn him."

"Bad idea," Mel said, shaking her head.

"At some point he's going to figure it out, you know. And I'd far rather have him think I was inexperienced than sucky."

Blythe snorted. "In this instance, *sucky* might be okay."

"Honestly, Blythe," Mel said, rolling her eyes. Then she laid a hand on April's knee. "Why don't you play it by ear? If it seems right to say something, then do it."

"There won't *be* any doing it if she does!"

"And maybe she has to go with her own gut."

"Guys! If I wasn't nervous before. I sure as heck am now!" April scrambled to her feet to look out the window again, tears springing to her eyes when she felt two sets of arms wrap around her.

Although, thankfully, the two women belonging to the arms had apparently said all they were going to say.

"But I don't wanna stay wif Aunt Frannie, I wanna stay wif you."

God, just kill him now. And that was before he let himself look into those big, brown, teary eyes.

A life of his own?

Sex?

On what planet?

Patrick had gone over and over it in his head, to the point where he had no idea anymore what was right and what wasn't. Whether all that "taking a shot" crap was based on anything more than being horny as hell, and how was that fair to anybody?

Good God, could he be any more conflicted? Here he'd finally reached the point where he felt okay about letting his libido out of the gate, allowing himself to fantasize about what might happen tonight—not that he was being presumptuous, but he was prepared—only to have reality hit him right between the eyes. That his life wasn't his own, and wouldn't be for some time to come.

"Go," his sister said, hauling his now trembly lipped daughter into her arms and facing him with a brook-no-argument stare.

"But—"

"*Now.* She'll survive, we'll survive. And believe it or not, you'll survive. So give Daddy a hug, sugar pie, and he'll see you in the morning."

At that, Lili sent up a wail like a tsunami siren, her sobs shattering his heart as he accepted her hug, then reluctantly turned and retreated down his sister's porch steps, Lili's "Daddy! *Daddy!*" following him like bereft puppies out to his truck.

Where he sat, feeling like total crap, until his brother-in-law rapped on the passenger-side window, making him jump. Blond, burly and affable as hell, Neil Solowicz was the kind of guy who never seemed to let anything faze him, not Patrick's bossy sister, not their four kids, nothing.

"Frannie's right, you know. She will get over it."

"Except, it's getting worse. All the times Lili's stayed here…" Patrick pushed out a breath. "It's like she knows."

Chuckling, his brother-in-law opened the door, climbed up to sit beside him and offered him a stick of gum, which Patrick took. They'd quit smoking at the same time, although Neil had fallen off the wagon at least twice that Patrick knew of.

"Yeah," Neil said, popping the gum into his mouth and folding his hands across his sweat-shirted belly, "kids definitely have a sixth sense about these things. Twerps can be zonked out for hours, but the minute we lock the bedroom door? Somebody's knocking, wanting to know what we're doing in there."

"Neil, for God's sake. Boundaries."

"Dude, we've got four kids. Not like how we got them is a secret. Or that I really, really like your sister."

A smile pushed at Patrick's mouth, followed by a sigh. "So what do you do? When they knock?"

"Give them a glass of water, send them back to bed and pick up where we left off."

"Really."

"Okay, some nights go more smoothly than others, but yeah. Pretty much."

"But how do you separate them from…that? In your head, I mean."

"I dunno, you just do. Or sometimes you don't. I mean, when I'm with the kids? It's not like I can always stop thinking about getting your sister alone. Sorry," he said when Patrick groaned. "Although when Frannie and I are… alone, I'm not thinking about the kids, believe me." He frowned. "You didn't figure this out when you were still with Natalie?"

"Obviously not. Since I'm *not* still with Nat."

"Good point. Look, not that I'm any expert on this or anything, but considering me and your sister are still going pretty strong after thirteen years—" he grinned "—and all those kids, let me just say this. Sure, your kid comes first. That makes you a good dad. That doesn't mean, however, that Lili gets to guilt you out of doing things for yourself. 'Cause the minute you give her that kind of power, you're screwed. Or, in this case, not. Dude…don't you dare let her hold you hostage." He looked out the windshield. "Or use her as an excuse."

"For what?"

"You know damn well what. Everything inside you's screaming to back out, am I right?"

"Not everything," Patrick breathed out after a moment. "But a lot. A helluva lot."

Wordlessly, Neil reached over to quickly squeeze Patrick's knee. Nearly ten years older than Patrick and having been with his sister since the ninth grade, sometimes he was more of a brother than Patrick's own brothers. And not nearly as inclined to give him crap.

He paused, then said, "I couldn't help but notice, when we were out at the inn for Thanksgiving, the way April looked at you. Like…" He laughed. "Like you were a puzzle she was gonna figure out if it killed her."

"And what if it does?" Patrick grumbled.

"Hey. You were the one who told me you found her hauling that fifteen-foot branch across the yard. Something tells me that one doesn't go quietly into that good night. So like Frannie said—" Neil pushed open the door, climbed out. "Go. Get outta here. Have *fun,* for cripe's sake." Hands in his pockets, he leaned inside the truck, his expression suddenly much more serious. "This could be a really good thing, Pat. Don't mess it up. And we promise to return your kid in more or less the same condition as we got her."

Neil slammed shut the door, giving a thumbs-up as Patrick drove off, his ambivalence riding shotgun—loud and obnoxious and constantly switching the radio between stations Patrick did not want to hear.

His obvious conflict practically bowled her over the instant she opened the door. Well, shoot. Because, her absurdly huge stash of condoms notwithstanding, she wasn't about to drag the man into her bed. In fact, judging by the look on his face right now, she'd be doing well to get him to the dining room.

Refusing to acknowledge the disappointment—or was that relief?—April plastered a smile on her face and said, "Come on in," and Patrick actually did, even if he mentally had one foot still on the other side of the door. She caught a whiff of winter marsh on his brown wool jacket, worn open over a beige corduroy shirt, a newer-looking pair of jeans—his attempt at making an effort, she thought with a smile that felt more genuine this time. She tried to imagine him in a suit, however, and failed miserably.

"You hungry?" she said, starting toward the dining room where a bevy of entrées and side dishes in chafing dishes awaited their critique. "Mel's been cooking half the day—we open for business next week—so we get to play guinea pigs tonight."

"We're staying in?"

She turned, catching herself when she tried to finger the phantom rings. "Seems a shame to waste all this food," she said mildly, even as she cringed at the trapped look in his eyes, the stiffness in his shoulders. "Patrick."

"What?"

"If you don't want to be here, then please leave. Because I am not holding up both ends of the conversation tonight."

"No, no…" His smile was so brief she almost missed it. "I'm here."

"You sure about that?"

He hauled in a breath big enough to make those shoulders rise an inch, held it for a good two or three seconds, then let it go. And if she caught the gonna-do-this-if-it-kills-me flash in his eyes…well. Far be it from her to stand in the man's way.

Or get out of his way, she thought when he started toward her, his eyes steady on her mouth, and whatever she'd been about to say flew right out of her head. Along with that earlier *Well, shoot.* Because that look in his eyes? Hoo, mama. No conflict there now, nope, none.

For the moment, anyway. Since she sincerely doubted he'd done a one-eighty in the past two days about not being able to see past tonight. Her crazily beating heart, however, was having none of it, pulsing in some very interesting places even before he reached her. Slowly, carefully, he threaded his still slightly chilled hands through her hair to cradle her head, then lowered his mouth to hers and kissed her boneless, and everything zinged and zapped she figured was supposed to be zinging and zapping, and she thought, tears stinging her eyes, *I want to make this man happy—*

She wanted to make him smile, and laugh, and act like a goofball. She wanted to wipe the doubt from his eyes, every last trace of it, to be the one person he'd know he could always count on. Always trust.

And if he made her happy in the process, that was okay, too.

But right now she knew this was *only* about this, and *that* was okay, too, they had to start somewhere. He pressed her spine against the doorjamb, lifting her, and she instinctively wrapped her legs around him, her arms around his neck, and kissed him back, hearing her own soft sounds of delight when their tongues touched, at how her breasts felt pressed against him, how he felt pressed against her... how the kisses went from tender to demanding and back to tender, how easy it was to follow his lead.

Yep, quick study, all right.

Still holding her, Patrick stopped, pushing out a short, embarrassed laugh before whispering, "Mel isn't here, I hope?"

April chuckled. "*Now* you ask this?"

"Got carried away."

"So I noticed."

"Can the food wait?"

"And if I said no...?"

He kissed her again. And again. And shifted her so she could feel exactly how carried away he was. Not that she'd had any personal experience with *carried away,* but again. Quick study. Not to mention enough romance novels to choke a horse.

"But you're not going to say no, are you?" he whispered. Hoarsely.

"Guess not," she said, laughing, her eyes burning again at his grin. A full-out grin, the grin of a man in the here-and-now. Then she took a breath.

"Um…"

"It's okay, I brought protection," Patrick said, letting her go. Only to sweep her into his arms, hard enough to make her bounce a little, to make her laugh again, and haul her across the gathering room, past the lobby, through her den and into her bedroom.

Where he came to a dead stop right inside the door.

So sue her, she'd been hopeful.

Not that there were strewn rose petals or anything. And the candles weren't even lit, since the house burning to the ground would've been a real mood killer. But—

"You turned down the sheets?" he said, still holding her.

She'd left on a single bedside lamp, so if things did go as planned, she wouldn't fall flat on her face stumbling to get to it. "Um, you know. Just in case."

He finally set her down. A little awkwardly, like somebody more used to hauling around bags of mulch and manure than people. People who weighed more than forty pounds, at least.

O-kay…now what?

Should she sit on the bed and strike a provocative pose? *Yeah, right.*

Start undressing? Start undressing *him?* Make the first move or wait for Patrick to do it? Light the candles?

Honestly, she was a half inch away from hyperventilating. Not exactly the modus operandi of a sexually experienced woman—

Wait. He was taking something out of his pocket, crossing to the bedside, tossing it—no, them—on the nightstand.

A moment before he leaned over to turn off the light.

April giggled. Like a fourteen-year-old. Gah—this kept getting better and better, didn't it? "Shouldn't we have lit the candles first?"

"No candles," she heard him say in the darkness, her

eyes slowly adjusting to the faint light coming through the window from the side yard's solar torches, her brain even more slowly clicking in to what he was saying. Or not saying.

"You want to do this in complete darkness— Oh!"

And there he was, right there in front of her, his hands on her sweater buttons, slowly undoing them. "If you don't mind."

She was about to say, heck, yeah, she minded—she'd always kind of thought when she finally had sex, she'd be able to see who she was having sex with. Just for kicks. Then again, this way he couldn't see her, either. Or more to the point, wouldn't be able to see all the "I have no idea what I'm doing!" faces she was probably going to make during the course of the evening. So on the whole, not necessarily a bad thing.

But even as she said, "Not at all," she realized *why* he wanted to do this in the dark, and her heart twisted…as did other things when, the sweater unbuttoned, he got to his knees to press a long, lazy kiss to her belly button, right above the waistband of her low-rider jeans. At her gasp, Patrick laughed. Against her belly.

Oh. Dear. Lord.

"You know what they say," he murmured. Between kisses. And gasps. Hers, not his. "When one sense is compromised, the others are heightened."

Man wasn't just whistling Dixie. Whoa. Then again—

April clamped her hands around his face and jerked it up, his confused, amused gaze barely visible in the dim light. "That means I can feel everything I can't see, too, you know."

"True, but—"

"Hush." Kneeling in front of him, she prayed her hands weren't trembling as much as they sure felt like they were as she started to unbutton his shirt. This was her! Undressing a man! In her bedroom!

"That I can see this—" she pushed aside the soft corduroy, immediately running into a broad swathe of puckered skin, shivering when he flinched "—as clearly as if there was a spotlight on it."

"It's not the same," Patrick whispered, his voice a little...strained. "Trust me."

"Maybe so, but..."

She stood, her heart thudding as she unhooked her bra and dropped it at his knees, her nipples instantly puckering in the chilly room. "You can't see me, either. Won't that be a problem?"

A laughing yelp escaped her throat when he grabbed her hand and yanked her down beside him on the thick, plush Chinese rug Blythe had picked for beside her bed, immediately cupping her bare breast to graze one rough finger across her nipple. "Not that I can tell," he said, the grin in his voice making her heart sing. Not to mention the wicked deliciousness of what he was doing to her breast. Granted, she was probably about the same color as the roses in the carpet, but since he couldn't see it, it was all good, right?

She returned the favor, skimming her fingers over the scarred tissue, only to frown when he flinched again.

"Does it hurt?" she asked, plucking back her hand.

"No." He took her hand, kissed it. Put it right back where it had been.

"Then why do you keep flinching?"

His laugh was low. "Why do you think?"

Okay, she might catch on yet. Hopefully before they both died of old age. She pressed her own kiss to his chest, then laid her cheek against it as she wrapped her arm around his rib cage, shoving aside his shirt, inhaling his scent. His strength and courage and goodness. Trying not to think of anything but that. "How long has it been," she asked quietly, "since you've been touched?" She lifted her face. "Like this, I mean?"

The heat kicked on, the draft like a caress. "Too long. You?"

She did a little flinching of her own. True, things seemed to be going pretty well, there didn't seem to be any reason to tell him. Wouldn't want to ruin the flow and all that. That said, neither did she want to outright lie...

"It feels like forever," she said, blowing out a sigh of relief when Patrick got to his feet, then hauled her to hers before leading her to the bed. Where he posthaste removed the rest of his clothes, then—with equal speed—removed the rest of hers, at which point it occurred to her he might not exactly be in the mood to go slow. Not after however many months it had been.

This could be an issue, since she had no idea if she was going be able to keep up. Or open up fast enough to not get hurt.

So tell him....

He pulled her against him, naked to naked, the sensation so incredible she might've passed out if she hadn't already been lying down.

Then he started to do things.

"What do you like?" he said, somehow kissing her, touching her, everywhere at once, and through the haze she thought, *Aw, thoughtful.*

"What you're, uh, doing right now—" whatever that was "—is great, thanks..."

Hel-lo, was he really going to...?

He really was.

And she was *really* going to let him, oh, yes she was, she thought, lifting her hips and basically—with an enormous sigh that made him laugh—giving in to The Force that was Patrick Shaughnessy's mouth. His warm, soft, amazing mouth. Which she could feel smiling against her.

Funny how she'd always thought she'd find this a little, well, awkward. If not embarrassing. Especially making these noises with an audience. But no. What this was, was…fun.

And becoming more fun by the second, the moans turning into pants…and she gasped, clutching at the bedclothes like she was going to fly off if she didn't, and then…*bam*.

Bammity-bam-bam-*BAM*.

Holy cow.

Patrick laughed, which is when April realized she'd said that out loud. Which is when she also realized—as her brain cells began to float back into place—that it was *her turn*. I mean, that was only fair, right? Except, um….

Hmm.

"Listen," he murmured into her ear, holding her close, "don't feel obligated to return the favor, I didn't do it for that reason."

"N-no?"

He chuckled. "Nope. I mean, if that floats your boat, fine. But if it doesn't, I'm sure we can figure out something else to keep us occupied. Although…" He kissed her hand, then pressed it to his chest again, "feel free to go where the spirit leads."

Man as Ouija board, heh, she thought, as she started to explore, frowning only briefly when she realized how much scarring there was, how much pain he had to have been in for so long. In a weird way, though, it gave her an out, that he'd think she was getting used to *his* body instead of getting used to a man's body, period. It was amazing, though, how quickly she picked up on his signals—*his* moans and sighs, the changes in his breathing patterns, his sighs of obvious pleasure. Heartened that she might be able to pull this off after all, she got bolder, touching places she'd never seen except in pictures or the occasional cable flick, amazed at how natural it felt, with the right person.

Oh, yeah, the spirit was leading, all right, his parts right into hers, if his flipping her onto her back was any indication. Not to mention the hardness of a certain body part which she'd made quite the close friend by now.

Although not as close as they were about to get, she thought, trying not to tense as he leaned over her, grabbing a condom off the nightstand. Oh, heck, what if he wanted her to put it on? She *knew* she should've picked up some bananas at the store…

She heard the package rip, some snapping—and grunting?—then he was between her legs, and again, instinct took over as she opened to him, almost crazy with anticipation from wanting him inside her.

And then he was, with a single thrust that caught her by surprise, making her cry out—and not in a good way—pushing him off her before she even knew she was doing it.

Chapter Eight

"Oh, Patrick…I am *so* sorry."

Her words barely registered.

Feeling like he'd been knocked clear into an alternate universe, Patrick sat on the edge of the bed, his mood—among other things—rapidly deflating. And it had been a good mood. The best damn mood he'd been in since he couldn't remember when. Her laughter, her no-holds-barred responses to his touch, the way she made him feel like nothing else mattered but what they were doing, right at that moment. To say it'd never been like that was an understatement. Except then, right before his mood got even better, she'd screamed, shoved him away. And in that split second afterward, he'd been horrified, confused, thinking it'd been too long, that in his eagerness to please her, to please both of them, he'd been too rough, he'd hurt her…

Another split second later, it hit him. That it hadn't been him.

"You're a virgin," he said dully into the darkness, too stunned to even be incredulous.

He heard her sigh. "Was. I think. Technically."

"How is that even possible! You were *married,* for cripes' sake…"

"Technically," she said again.

He turned to see she was backed against the headboard, facing the window with the sheet bunched at her breasts, and he silently swore. Yeah, he still felt like he'd been clobbered with a baseball bat, but in hindsight, there'd been clues, hadn't there? That he'd had to show her where—and how—to touch him, a certain…amazement in her reactions, like someone seeing the ocean for the first time. But in the back of his mind—way in the back, thinking hadn't been his top priority right then—he'd chalked it up to them being new together. Or that'd it been a while since her husband.

Then she lifted the edge of the sheet to wipe her cheek, and chagrin flooded through him, diluting the frustration. If not the confusion.

He reached for her hand, his heart constricting when she grabbed his back. "Are you okay?" he asked, wishing she'd look at him. More than half glad she didn't. "Did I hurt you?"

She licked her lips. "It was…a surprise. I thought I was ready. I mean, I wanted…" Her eyes squeezed shut, then opened again. "I must've tensed or something…it wasn't your fault. I'm sorry," she whispered again on a little sob, shaking her head. "That was stupid, I should've listened to my instincts and told you. But the girls said…"

"The girls? Your cousins, you mean?" When she nodded, he pressed, "The girls said what? That it was better *not* to tell me?"

Another nod. "They said you'd freak."

"Like I'm not freaking now?"

Finally, she looked at him. "You don't sound like you're freaking."

No, he'd done that before, hadn't he? When he'd insisted on doing this in the dark. Because if they hadn't, he probably would've picked up on those clues, seen in her face that something wasn't right. So how could he fault her for not being totally honest with him?

Patrick shut his eyes. Damn. "So…that, uh, other thing we did. Was that—?"

"What can I say, it's a night of firsts."

Exhaling loudly, he stood, patting the nightstand for the box of matches he'd seen before they turned out the light. The box found, he opened it, her soft, surprised gasp that he'd changed his mind barely louder than the whoosh of the match when he struck it.

"What are you doing?" she said when he touched the flame to the already burned wick on the scented candle, then another, and another, until the room gently pulsed with the warm glow.

"Shedding a little light on things," he said, shaking out the match and pinching the tip with his fingers to make sure it was out before tossing it in the trash can on the other side of the stand.

"Turn around," she said gently.

He did, his hands curled at his hips. Nobody had seen him naked since Natalie, when he'd been dumb enough to think it wouldn't matter to her. That as his wife, she'd pledged to stick by him, be with him, no matter what. Right?

With obvious relish, April's eyes slowly grazed his body, inch by inch, a smile gradually curving her lips.

"Go ahead, take your time, I'm in no hurry," he said, and she laughed.

"Can't help it. You're beautiful."

"April, don't—"

"I'm serious." Then she held out her hand and whispered, "Get over here."

Patrick hesitated, then climbed back into the bed to take her in his arms, laying his cheek on top of her rumpled hair. A large part of him wanted to believe he was only being kind. Or that she was. But another part—the part he didn't want to hear from—knew it was more than that. That he was here because he wanted to be here, that holding her felt good. That he felt genuinely bad about what had happened, and not only because *he'd* been gypped.

"I still can't believe...that you and your husband...?"

"Nope."

"*Why,* for Pete's sake?"

"It's a long story. Which I really don't feel like talking about right now. Suffice it to say we had an unconventional marriage."

"Ya think?" When she sighed, he said, "Did you know this going in? That you wouldn't—"

"Yes."

"And you actually agreed?"

"I did." She paused. "In writing, even."

He remembered her...enthusiasm, those sweet little sounds she made in her throat, her *joy*...

How could she have willingly denied that part of herself?

Why not? You have.

"Are you angry?" she whispered, shattering his thoughts.

He thought. "Now that I'm mostly over the shock...no. Although it occurs to me if you'd warned me, I would have done things, well, differently."

"Really?" She lifted her head to look up at him. "Not run off screaming into the night?"

"Once we were naked? Probably not."

"I see," she said, and he chuckled.

"What can I say, timing is everything."

At his own words, Patrick shut his eyes, glad April couldn't see the ambivalence crawling back out of the dark corners of his mind, nipping at his fragile peace. A large part of him did want to run, to get out of here while he still could. Before this gal wrapped herself around his damaged heart as tightly as she'd wrapped her legs around his hips, when he'd lifted her up in the hallway. All that trust…that *giving*…he couldn't handle it.

And yet, he couldn't bring himself to leave her, not yet, not until he knew she was okay.

His stomach muscles jumped when that soft, smooth hand trailed over his abs, then lower. Not quite to bull's eye but close enough to get things stirring again.

Figuring this time—if, indeed, that's what this was—it would be nice if they were both on the same page, he grabbed her hand, holding it flat against his belly.

"What are you doing?"

She paused, then slipped her hand out from under his and continued her journey. "Finishing what I started?"

He sucked in a breath. Shut his eyes. He forced out, "You don't have to do th-that—"

"Just hush and show me what to do."

So he did, forcing himself to watch her face as he tutored her, almost laughing when her brow puckered in concentration. Suddenly, she stopped, shaking her head, and he almost cried.

"What are you—"

"Get another condom. Now."

Again, it took a moment for the words to register. Then he was frantically slapping the nightstand for the packet—

"Can't find it—"

He felt a brisk breeze as he heard the sheet whip back. "Top drawer."

Thinking, *You have condoms?* Patrick yanked open the drawer so hard the whole thing came out, scattering little foil packets all over the floor like an X-rated piñata. He stared, momentarily transfixed. "How many guys were you expecting?"

"They were for you, I didn't know what to get, just *pick something, for Pete's sake!*"

One quick riffle later, he was suited up and ready to go, only to have his breath leave his lungs when he turned to find April on her back.

In-freaking-credible.

He knelt over her, stroking her hair off her cheek, now realizing the real reason why he'd wanted to make love in the dark before—not so she couldn't see him, but so he couldn't see her. Couldn't see the trust, the ingenuousness. Because if he couldn't see it, it couldn't get inside him, could it?

Too late, he thought as he said, "I'm going to go real slow, okay? You let me know if—"

"Got it." Her eyes squeezed closed. "Just…go."

"Not until you relax."

"Relax. Okay." He saw her take in a breath, let it slowly out. Still with her eyes shut.

"Look at me, sweetheart," he said, even as the "sweetheart" ricocheted in his brain. Her eyes popped open, and he laughed. "Are you sure…?"

"Yes, sorry. Although I think it was easier when I didn't know what was about to happen."

"Shh…" He stretched out over her, holding her hands

in his as he kissed her, about to go crazy from her scent as he gently sucked at her neck, then her breasts, until her breathing changed and he knew she was in The Zone.

"You good?" he asked, getting a drowsy, "Mmm-hmm," in response.

He lifted her knees, positioned himself, said a prayer. For what, he wasn't sure.

"Look at me," he commanded again, his heart stuttering when she did. Inch by exquisitely agonizing inch, he slid into her, watching her face for signs of whatever she might not be inclined to admit. At one point she tensed, only to immediately shake her head.

"No, it's fine, I'm okay…oh…" Another inch. And another long, breathy, "Ohhh…"

He retreated. Gently pushed forward again. Farther, this time. April sighed, and smiled, her eyes drifting closed again.

He kissed her. "Close?"

"Shh," she whispered, wrapping herself around him, taking him in. Smiling.

Holding him still.

There should be a medal for this, he thought, sweat beading on his brow from holding back. Then she sighed again and mumbled, "Go," and he felt like a horse let out of the starting gate, except one push and over she went, panting and laughing and crying and carrying him right along with her.

Right into enemy territory.

His slice of pecan pie finished, Patrick set his empty plate on the coffee table, slightly startling April when he then stretched out on her couch to lay his head on her lap, claiming her hand to toy with her fingers as he stared into the fire.

Yes, they'd finally gotten around to eating—Patrick in his pants and shirt, April in her pale blue fleece robe and what she strongly suspected was rampant sex hair—although April had been a trifle distracted, what with glowing so much and all. Not distracted enough, however, that she hadn't put away more food in the past half hour than she had all week. According to her cousins, sex was supposed to *diminish* your appetite. Not in this case, April thought with a smile as she stroked Patrick's short, bristly hair. When the endorphins wore off she was probably gonna be a little sore. Ask her if she cared.

And you know something else? She had a really strong suspicion this would not have been nearly so much fun when she was a teenager. Especially since her partner would have most likely been a teenage boy. And for all Blythe's smug "Nyah-nyah-nyah, I did it first," truth be told her cousin hadn't sounded all that thrilled about the "doing" part of things.

"I suppose you're gonna tell your cousins all about this?" he said, and she laughed.

"That I'm a big girl now? I think they're going to guess that part. But the details? Not if they tied me up and tortured my bare feet with feathers."

She felt the rumble of his chuckle beneath her palm. "Wouldn't put it past them."

"Neither would I. But I won't break. Promise."

He arched to look up at her, then lifted his hand to the back of her head to pull her down for a kiss, whispering, "I'm sure you won't," when he was done.

What is going through your head right now, Patrick Shaughnessy?

Oh, they'd cuddled, and kissed, and exchanged what she assumed were the standard postcoital pleasantries. She'd thanked him—with every scrap of sincerity she could dredge up while still limp as a dishrag—and he'd said, "No problem," with a ridiculously huge grin on his face, which tickled her immensely. Then he'd insisted she soak for a while in a hot bath—which tickled her even more— while he fixed them plates of food. In other words, as far as first times went? On a scale of one to ten, hers was well in the double digits.

Still, even though he was doing and saying all the "right" things, April could sense he wasn't nearly as relaxed as he would have her believe. As though he was trying *too* hard, maybe? She also kept thinking she needed to say something to reassure him, somehow, but Lord alone knew what that might be.

And that was even before she'd finally finished telling him about her marriage. He'd listened while she'd talked, frowning into his food, mostly, but not saying much. Already she'd figured out he needed time to process things. Which apparently included when, or even if, to open up to her the same way.

The good news was…he was still here. That he hadn't bolted, that he had listened, that he was now lying here with his head in her lap, gave her hope. A foolish, foundationless hope, maybe, but hope nonetheless.

Because she thought she might be falling in love. Not that she'd ever say this to Patrick. Lord, no. Not yet, at any rate. Because *of course* it was too early—to be thinking it, let alone saying it—even she knew that. And she wasn't entirely sure that wasn't the hormones talking, since if you asked her right now to tell you why she thought she was falling, she couldn't have begun to tell you why. All she knew was, she'd never felt like this before. That whatever this was, it was over and above what she'd called "love" up to this point.

But that thing about wanting to make him happy? To

do whatever she could to see that grin again? And again and again and again?

Probably isn't going away anytime too soon, nope.

He curled forward to sit up and face the fire, propping the soles of his feet on the edge of the coffee table before swinging his arm over her shoulders and drawing her close. "I know I've been kind of quiet, but that's just me turning things over in my head. And somewhere along the line it occurred to me what a big deal it was, you trusting me like that. Can't say as I understand why, to be honest, but you did. That was a huge step you took, and you took it with me, and, well, I guess I'm still kind of shocked."

"Silly goober," she said, and he softly laughed.

"My point is, though, that I got to thinking…the least I could do is trust you back. As much as I'm able to, anyway. And I suppose you're curious." He paused. "About what happened."

"Your mother already—"

"She wasn't there, April," he said, and she thought she'd crumble inside.

Nestling against his chest, she slipped her hand inside his shirt, the scarring already familiar, almost reassuring in a weird sort of way. "I'm not sure *curious* is the right word. I only want to know if you want to tell me. I want to know…" She cleared her throat, sending up a silent prayer for the right words. "I want to know *whatever* you want to tell me. But I won't pry, I promise. Or push. And if I do, tell me it's off-limits and I'm good with that."

"Really?"

"Let's put it this way—I promise to try my best to be good with it. How's that?"

"Deal," he said, kissing the top of her head. He took his sweet time, though, cranking up, to the point that April wondered if he'd changed his mind. Then, at last, he said,

"My gut instinct, afterward, was to shut down. Talking about it—what I remembered, anyway, a large chunk of that day is still missing in my brain—was the last thing I wanted to do. Took at least three therapists to get it through my head that was not the way to go. Crap happens to everybody. But you can't deal with it by repressing the memories. I'd convinced myself…"

He paused, then released a breath in her hair. "That I was too tough to grieve. That admitting how lost and angry and resentful I felt was a sign of weakness. Because those feelings scared the bejeezus out of me."

She thought of his mother's words. Realized, at that moment, that perhaps her mission wasn't only about bringing him joy, but about giving him permission to *feel*. To be human, for heaven's sake. "They scare the bejeezus out of everybody, honey."

"Took me a while to accept that, though. That said… other than my last therapist and my family, I haven't talked about this to anyone."

"Not even your ex-wife?"

"I tried to, believe me. She didn't want to hear. Said she didn't want all that 'negativity' poisoning the atmosphere." At April's silence, Patrick said, "No comment?"

"None that a good Southern girl should be making," she said, and he smiled, kissed her hand.

She then listened in silence as he told her about the explosion, the fire, his momentary awareness of complete chaos as adrenaline and instinct took over, before everything went black. About waking up in the hospital in Germany to his mother standing over him, the tears in her eyes giving the lie to her smile. About having no recall of rescuing his teammates, the agony of realizing who hadn't made it. The months of treatment that followed, the painful surgeries and treatments, the constant battle against discouragement and depression. And guilt, no matter how often he'd been reminded of the men he'd saved. The number of times he'd seriously considered ending it all.

"Then I'd remember I had a daughter. A little girl I'd hardly ever seen. Nat could've brought her to San Antonio, but she didn't want to 'traumatize' her. And maybe, at that point, she was right, I don't know…"

He released another breath. "At least she sent me pictures and videos. I mean, I loved Lili anyway, she was my kid. But getting to see her smile, and her first step… it didn't matter how little I'd seen her in the flesh, I still would've killed for that kid, you know? So, yeah, she's what kept me going. Guess I figured, since I hadn't died, God wasn't letting me off the hook yet. That Lili was waiting for me. Counting on me." Another pause. "I just had no idea how much."

"You mean because your wife…?"

"Left me, yeah. Left both of us. Last spring, after I'd been home three, four months. Funny thing was, Lili was fine with her daddy not looking 'normal.' Her mother, however…she never could come to terms with it. Although I have to say…"

Patrick lowered his feet to the floor, removing his arm from around April's shoulders to lean forward, his hands clasped between his knees. "All the talking, the therapy…it brought me back from the brink of hell, sure. But it couldn't fix what was broken inside me."

Gently, April laid her palm between his shoulder blades. "You think you're broken?"

He scrubbed a hand down his face. "I know I am, April. Even when things feel almost good again, nothing feels the same. *I* don't feel the same. I don't mean about how I look, although the stares still catch me off guard sometimes. But being over there, seeing what I saw, seeing my men…"

She saw his jaw clench, even as she felt him shudder underneath her hand. "It took a helluva bigger toll than I had any idea it would when I signed up as a wet-behind-the-ears nineteen-year-old. I'm not sure anybody ever comes to terms with that. Not completely."

He twisted to look into her eyes, the frustrated expression in his tearing her to pieces. "Tonight, being with you... I can't even describe it. It almost felt, I don't know..." He faced the fire again, his head shaking. "Real."

She stilled, hardly daring to breathe. "But that's good, right?"

"I said it *felt* real," he said softly. "That doesn't mean it was."

Her eyes swimming, April wrapped her arm around his back and laid her head on his shoulder. "It sure as heck was real for me," she whispered, then smiled. "Twice." When he snorted a laugh in return, she said, "And if that's your way of saying this was a one-shot deal, I'm going to be *very* pissed."

Now he barked out a laugh, before turned to cup her face in his hands. "Even if I say things are never going to change? That I can never give you all of myself because I'm barely able to scrape enough together to give to my kid?"

She thought, weighing her options. Could she handle another conditional relationship? Was she a fool for even considering putting off her life again—putting off "real"—after she already had for so long? And it wasn't as if she didn't know that loving a man didn't pave the way to changing him. For sure it hadn't worked for her mother with her father, and she wasn't so much of a fool as to believe it would work with Patrick.

And if it hadn't been for that *hope* singing and dancing and bouncing around inside her head, she might've made what most folks would call the right decision. She was tough, she knew that, but still—she'd never ceded that kind of power to another human being. Clay's death had stung, yes, but Patrick's rejection…that could potentially devastate her.

But giving up without trying would devastate her far more.

Because then she'd be giving up on Patrick, wouldn't she? Exactly like his wife had.

April clumsily shifted to straddle his lap, the heat from the fire licking at her bare back as she let the robe slide off and linked her hands behind his neck. Patrick's eyes immediately darkened, and April realized she didn't feel like a hussy, brazen or otherwise. What she felt like, was a woman. A woman relishing being able to give whatever she had to her man.

For as long as he needed it.

"What you are, right now," she whispered, teasing his mouth with hers, "is more than I've ever had before. The thought of giving this up when I just found it…" Softly, she kissed him again. "Now how much sense does that make?"

When he didn't answer, she levered off his lap, trying not to trip over the robe, then held out her hand. Wordlessly he rose and took it, leading her back to the bedroom.

No, she definitely wasn't going to be able to walk tomorrow. But inside her head, she'd be dancing like nobody's business.

Chapter Nine

The next morning April scurry-waddled through the house, pulling her barely combed hair into a ponytail as she tried to focus on her long to-do list for the day: potential employees to interview, decorations to finish, her mother's call to return. Because didn't it figure the woman *would* call on the one night when answering the phone hadn't been on the top of her list? At least Mama had said it wasn't urgent, she just wanted to chat, which marginally mitigated the guilt factor.

She veered into the kitchen, yelping right along with Blythe, who, seated at the island, jumped and shoved down her laptop lid at April's entrance.

"Damn, girl—give a person a heart attack, why not?"

"You should talk!" Pulse throbbing, April passed her cousin and headed straight for the Keurig. "What are you doing here?"

Blythe took a bite of something obviously left over from

the night before. As usual, she'd taken casual chic to the next level—velvet leggings, four-inch-high ankle boots, a half-dozen random necklaces somehow not smothering at least three cleverly layered tops. "Potential new client, some moneybags couple out near where Ryder's parents live. Saw pics of the inn on my website, asked if they could see it in person before deciding whether to hire me or not. Hope you don't mind?"

"Letting you parade rich people through here?" April dropped her coffee selection into the basket, shut the lid. "Not hardly."

Twisting to face April, Blythe propped one elbow on the island countertop and took a swallow of coffee. "So how was it? Not that I really need to ask, your hair is a disaster and you're wearing two different shoes."

April glanced down. Yep. One ballet flat with a buckle, one with a bow. At least they were both black. But still.

Patrick had left around midnight. Reluctantly, April thought, but still needing space to digest what had happened. Still torn. "It was good," she said, deciding to flip the track switch on the conversation. "Why'd you close your laptop so fast when I came in?"

"What? Uh, nothing. Just a startled reflex." Except April caught the blush, signifying her cousin wasn't telling all. Which didn't stop Blythe's squint. "And don't even think about changing the subject."

"Watch me."

Blythe rolled her pretty periwinkle eyes. "But I'm right, yes? Not that I'm pressing for details…"

"Press all you like, I'm not giving any."

Although whether or not she and Patrick would ever fool around again, she had no clue. Would be a crying shame, though, letting all those condoms go to waste….

"So," she said brightly. "When are these clients coming? I've got two interviews this morning and then Patrick's picking me up to go get the tree."

"At nine. And you're picking out Christmas trees together? Dude."

"He has a truck. It seemed expedient."

"Is his kid going to be there?"

Ah, yes. That. Or perhaps she should say, that, *too.*

April poured herself a bowl of Cheerios, slicing a banana into it before climbing on the stool beside her cousin. "I have no idea," she said softly, pouring milk into the bowl, watching all those little life preservers jostling for space as they floated to the top.

"Oops. That doesn't sound good."

"No," she said, clinking the spoon a couple of times against the edge of the bowl before shoveling her first spoonful into her mouth. Milk escaped; she grabbed a napkin to catch it before it dribbled down her chin. "It doesn't."

"Meaning?"

While what she and Patrick had shared in bed was not open for discussion, April could definitely use another perspective on one or two other things. Especially since, between sleep deprivation and hormonal overindulgence, the temptation to jump to conclusions was through the roof.

"I'm not sure." April took another bite. One not quite so goopy. "I get the feeling Patrick is afraid to let me get close to Lili. Or her, me."

"It is pretty early, you know," Blythe said gently. "So can you blame him?"

"Not really," April breathed out. "Especially considering what happened with his ex. Lili almost never sees her mother. And when she does, Patrick said she's wrecked for days, which in turn wrecks *him.* So, since…"

April's throat closed against the threatening tears, as

the reality of the situation smacked her between the eyes. Clear light of day and all that.

"So since this is only a passing thing…"

Shoot. Pinching her mouth together, April dropped the spoon into her bowl and sat back, her arms tightly folded over her stomach. Blythe wrapped her hand around April's wrist.

"You sure about that?"

"I'm not sure about anything. Not even how I feel, to be honest. Yes, I know—it's been like five minutes, what's the rush?" She sighed. "Although I do see potential, at least. He doesn't."

"He's a guy. They never do."

"*Some* guys must, else nobody would ever get married."

"I think they simply get tired of fighting," her cousin said on a short, dry laugh.

April frowned at her cousin. "Men do fall in love. Look at Ryder with Mel," she said before Ms. Cynical could protest.

"Okay, I'll give you that one. But if Patrick…" Blythe pressed her lips together, then opened her laptop again, quickly clicking away from whatever had been on the screen.

"Spit it out, Blythe."

A moment passed before she met April's gaze, her own full of concern. "You don't want a man to be with you simply because you wore him down. I've been there. And ultimately that hurts far more than if the relationship had never gotten off the ground to begin with. You also…"

"What?"

"You're very new at this. So just be careful, okay? Protect your own heart first. Don't give until you've bled yourself dry. Because trust me, they don't appreciate it."

It wasn't as if April didn't hear her cousin. Or, heck,

even agree with her, to a certain extent. She *was* new at this, she was vulnerable, and heaven knew she'd always been predisposed to giving of herself without thinking through the consequences. Except this time, even if she didn't really know what she was doing, she did know what the risks were. And what the rewards could be...if she was willing to take that chance—

"And you know what?" Blythe said, derailing April's thoughts. "Kudos to Patrick for putting his daughter first. Maybe if more parents did that we wouldn't have so many screwed up kids in the world." The doorbell rang. Muttering, "Probably my clients," she dismounted the stool, tossing, "You should probably fix yourself up," over her shoulder as she strode from the room.

Very true.

Ten minutes later, hair tamed and shoes matching, April answered the door herself, smiling for the grinning couple on the other side, there to interview for the housekeeper/ handyman positions. The house echoed with their oohs and aahs as she ushered the two men—one, a bearded blond, the other with skin like oiled teak—to her office.

Heh. Somewhere, Nana's ashes were whirling like a dust devil.

Patrick parked in front of the inn and got out, his sensitive skin protesting some in the damp breeze as he stood with his hands rammed in his work coat pockets, half wondering if last night had been a dream. A good one, for a change. The corners of his mouth stretched: A *very* good one.

The front door swung open and April hustled through it, her smile knocking his breath—not to mention coherent thought—clean out of him.

Literally shaking off the dizziness, Patrick walked

around to the truck's passenger side to open the door as she approached, her hair bouncing off her shoulders, a bright blue scarf wound in some bizarre way across her chest. No one else was around that he could tell, no other cars besides hers parked in the driveway—

"Hi," she said when she reached him, not quite shyly but close enough to make his throat catch, to send a hundred memories from the night before shooting through him, instantly provoking both tenderness and an arousal so intense he nearly choked. As it was he'd lain awake the rest of the night, head propped on one arm, staring at his shadowy ceiling and trying to make sense of what had happened. What he'd gotten himself into. What, he now realized when she stood on tiptoe to gently press her mouth to his, he wasn't getting himself out of anytime too soon.

Or—and here was the frightening part—wanted to.

He bent to haul her close so he could kiss her properly, feeling all warm inside when she laughed against his lips. Even so—even now—the impulse to run was so strong he nearly shook with it, never mind that all he wanted was to carry her back into the house and bury himself, and his pain, inside all that sweetness and generosity for as long as she'd let him—

Damn. He was so hard it hurt.

April laughed again, a soft, low chuckle. "Guess that answers my question."

He set her down. "And what question would that be?"

"Whether you want to, you know. Again. With me."

Never before had he found coyness even remotely a turn-on. Until now. Probably because with April, it was genuine. Like everything else about her.

"Wanting to, *you know,* again was never a question. Whether I *should* was something else entirely."

She met his gaze straight on, the coyness banished. "So who are you trying to protect?"

"I'm not sure."

Huffing an obviously frustrated sigh, she poked her hands in her jacket pockets and looked away, like she was thinking, before eyeing him again.

"Then maybe you need to clear that up in your head," she said, firmly enough but not meanly. Although he doubted she could do "mean" if you put a gun to her head. "Because here's my take on it—if you feel you have to protect yourself, then fine. Go. Right now," she said, pointing to the road. "But I don't need protecting, Patrick Shaughnessy, from you or anybody else. I invited you into my bed because I wanted you there." She flushed. "And I'm inviting you back because I *still* want you there. Because I waited a heckuva long time to find a man I wanted to do that with, and frankly, I think I made a dang good choice. It was fun, *you* were fun, and like I said, I'm not hot on the idea of quitting before I've hardly gotten started. So if it's all the same to you—"

"Good God, woman, you talk a lot."

Grinning, she freed one hand to grab the front of his jacket, like she'd done in the car a few nights ago. "And something tells me you can probably figure out how to shut me up."

Unable to decide if she was a torment or a blessing, Patrick palmed the truck's roof. "What about the Christmas tree?"

Now the grin was downright sassy. "Somehow I doubt they're gonna sell out in the next hour."

Sometime later, watching April bop from tree to tree in Sam's lot like a demented Energizer Bunny, Patrick realized that whereas some women got drowsy after sex, it apparently had the opposite effect on the one he'd made cry out twice in twenty minutes.

And talk? Yowsa. The woman had practically gabbed his ear off on the ride over—about the couple she'd hired who were going to be absolutely *perfect,* she already loved them to bits, about how she still hoped her parents would come for Christmas, about how Mel and she were going to have a booth set up in the town square for the festival to drum up business. Gal always had been bubbly, but now she was fizzing over like a can of warm soda.

And I did that, he thought with a slight jolt to his midsection—

"Come hold this one for me so I can see what it looks like," she said, wrestling with a nine-foot Noble fir partially tangled with a bunch of its cousins.

Patrick ambled over, feeling kind of fizzy himself, truth be told. Not to mention more mellow than he'd been in a long, long time. And if the shadows hadn't been banished entirely, at least they'd become porous enough for the light to work through in places. He grabbed the tree, easily yanking it upright, unable to hold in his grin as he watched April give it a slow, careful once-over, looking a lot like Lili when she was concentrating on something or other. A thought that clawed at his brain like a pesky mutt wanting inside, how much April and Lili would hit it off.

If he let them.

"Put it in the 'maybe' pile over there," April said, waving toward a growing collection of trees that'd made her short list. April had many fine qualities—*many* fine qualities—but making snap decisions was not among them. By rights, Patrick mused as he plunked the tree up against the chain-link fencing segregating the trees by type and height, he should've been at least moderately irritated by now. That he wasn't probably had a lot to do with the sex.

A lot, but not all.

He thought of how Natalie had always been complaining, always unhappy, always looking at him like he was to blame for everything that had gone wrong in her life. And damned if he hadn't bought into the whole gloomy picture. The few times they had made love after his return—although using that term for what they'd done was a stretch—her heart had not only clearly not been in it, it'd been nowhere to be found. Sex had been a chore, something she'd had to endure, not enjoy. Even when he'd brought her to climax, it was almost like she somehow resented it—

"One more," April said, pointing to her next candidate. "And then I'll choose." She clasped her hands to her chest, eyes sparkling. "I promise."

Patrick laid hold of the tree, turning it when she signaled, thinking how different April was from his ex. Like, from-a-previously-undiscovered-planet different. To be that positive, that loving, despite everything she'd been through…frankly, it was pretty humbling. And reason whined again that not only was it dumb, keeping April and Lili apart, it was downright selfish.

Beaming, she clapped her hands. "This is it! This is our tree!"

"You sure?"

"Of course I'm sure." At what must've been his skeptical look, she laughed. "Okay, so maybe it takes me a while to make up my mind. But once I do, I do not change it."

"No buyer's remorse, huh?" Patrick said as he hefted the tree, trekked to the cash register.

She went ahead of him, tugging her wallet out of her purse before giving him a confident look that brought the shadows scuttling back. "Nope. Never," she said, and he thought, *She's glowing, dumbass, because this is all new to her. That she "picked" you is pure happenstance.*

His mellow, now pierced, started to evaporate. Not completely, but enough to see through it. To see that what he wanted—to hang on to this moment forever—was, and always would be, at odds with reality.

Talk about dumb.

See, eventually April would wake up. And when she did she'd realize her journey had barely begun, that Patrick was by no means the last stop on the line. For now, though, he'd take the moment. Enjoy the hell out of it, do whatever he could to keep smiles on both their faces. When it was over, it was over. No regrets.

But *that's* why he had to keep Lili and April apart. Because he could handle the end, when it came.

To do that to his kid, though, would be downright cruel.

Over the next week, April found herself alternately grinning like an idiot and fighting off a recurring funk that came dangerously close to anger.

The grinning stemmed from the irrefutable fact that she and Patrick were now lovers. Perhaps not as frequently as either of them might like—between the inn's being officially open for business, his work schedule and his daddy obligations, logistics were a nightmare—but the man was nothing if not determined. And surprisingly creative. Give him thirty minutes, the back of his pickup and a sleeping bag, and…

April grabbed a brochure from beside the computer on the registration desk and fanned herself.

So. Anyway. That part of things was going great. The man was considerate and attentive and oh-so-eager to please. And—when he let his guard down—funny. He was even talking more, praise be. But his being clearly dead-set against her being around his daughter…that needled. Not for the obvious reasons, though. She couldn't fault him for wanting to protect Lili—that was one of the things she found so appealing, for goodness' sake.

But.

It was also pretty clear that as long as he refused to let her into that part of his life—the most important part, as it should be—she had no hope of becoming a *real* part of his life. The sex was great, she loved the sex, she was more grateful than she could say for the sex…but that wasn't a relationship.

And it was quite obvious that Patrick was deliberately keeping this thing between the sheets—or inside a sleeping bag—so they *wouldn't* develop a relationship.

Which is what was worrisome. Not to mention roused some very strong suspicions that Patrick was denying himself far more than he was denying April. *That's* what made her want to slap the doofus six ways to Sunday…even as it strengthened her resolve to stick it out, to work with what she was given—in this case, sex—until she saw that speck of light through some chink or other in his armor that showed her the way inside.

All in good time, she thought, breathing deeply as Todd, who along with his partner, Michael, now lived in the house's downstairs back bedroom, plugged in the vacuum cleaner to do one final sweep before the day's guests arrived. Already they'd proved themselves godsends, their conscientious attention to detail earning April's undying respect. Not to mention gratitude. Minutes into their interview, she'd known that she and the pair of thirtysomethings—one a musician, the other a watercolor artist—had been destined to be together. However, Todd in particular was both uncannily intuitive and empathetic, which meant hiding anything from the brawny blond was an exercise in futility.

In fact, pale brows now hiked over hazel eyes riddled

with concern. And she had no doubt about what. Although she'd said nothing to either of them about Patrick, they'd seen her with him enough—and knew enough about Patrick's situation by the sheer dint of living in the same town—to draw a conclusion or six.

"Everything okay?" Todd said, pretending to rearrange the vacuum cord, move furniture that didn't need to be moved.

"Couldn't be better," April chirped. "You get the goody baskets up in the rooms yet?"

"An hour ago, and you, honey, are a terrible liar. Pardon me for saying this, but you look like you're about to fall over."

She sort of laughed. "Would it help to say at least it's a good tired? But it has been a lot busier than I expected for barely getting our doors open." And at least he hadn't zeroed in on her musings. Bad enough that her cousins both read her like a billboard. Leave it to her to hire employees who were every bit as bad. Or good. Whatever.

Todd wagged his head. "Didn't Michael and I tell you from the beginning, anytime you want to take some time for yourself, we're more than happy to inn-sit? And since we'd both very much like to hang on to this job for more than five minutes, we're hardly going to do anything to screw it up."

"Ohmigosh, you think I don't trust you? No, that's not it, not it at all. It's…"

"You're not ready to leave your baby with some stranger. I know. Only putting it out there. As an option." Finally he turned back to the vacuum. "Especially if you ever expect to get some alone time with your strapping young man. Just saying."

The vacuum roared to life before she could respond. *Creep,* she thought, her eyes stinging.

She felt her cell phone buzz in her pocket—her mother. To get away from the noise she went into the office, shutting the door behind her.

"Just checking to see how things were going," Mama said. "Although I imagine it'll be slow at first, until word gets out."

April could never quite tell these days whether her mother's comments stemmed from genuine maternal support or latent passive aggression. Not that it was any secret Mama expected the venture to fail. You know, because the economy was so shaky, and it was rare for a new business to make it past the first year, blah-blah-blah. Which begged all manner of eye rolls, considering what April's father had put her mother through. Then again, she supposed one could be an enabler and still have full cognizance of what you were enabling. And heaven knew if anyone understood how few ventures actually thrived, it would be her mother.

"Actually, things are going really well," she said, walking to the window to gaze out over the now more-or-less recovered front grounds. "I've already got bookings through January—"

"Really?"

"Really. And the restaurant's taking off, Mel's doing a fantastic job with that."

Oh, and by the way? I've taken a lover....

"Did you get the pictures I sent? Of the house and grounds?" she said after swallowing down the giggle threatening to erupt.

"Um, yes. We did."

"So what did you think? Gorgeous, huh?"

After a long pause, her mother said, "I'll admit, I wouldn't have recognized the place. Blythe's very talented, isn't she?"

"She is that. And the room done up in greens and blues? That's where I thought you and Dad could stay when you come for Christmas—"

"April, honey…nothing's changed. About how I feel, I mean. You can't wallpaper over the memories, no matter how hard you try. And besides, I thought you said you were booked through January."

"No, I said I have bookings through January. There are still openings." She fisted her hand, feeling her nails bite into her palm. "And I'm holding that room for you."

"Why in heaven's name would you do that?"

"Because…" *Oh, just say it, for heaven's sake.* "Because I'm an eternal optimist who still believes that one day her mother will stop letting a dead woman control her?"

She heard Mama suck in a breath. "You have no idea, the things she said to me, to all three of us—"

"No, I don't. And frankly, I don't care. Not that she hurt you, I don't mean that, but because she's *gone,* and the house is *mine,* and I want you to be proud of me for what I've done with it. To at least support what I'm trying to do as much as you used to with Dad! After all, considering what I gave up for you, it's the least you could do!"

April slapped a hand to her mouth. Why she'd chosen now to come clean, she couldn't say. Actually, yes, she could, since now she *knew* what she'd given up. And she didn't only mean the deliciousness of a rough-fingered caress across her sensitive skin, the feel of being wrapped in a man's arms, or orgasms so intense they achieved out-of-body-experience status. Of kisses that went on forever, negating the need for words. No, what she'd given up was being able to give of her whole self, to hold and touch someone *else,* to give someone *else* those out-of-body experiences. To heal the pain in someone's eyes, even if only occasionally—

"April! What on *earth* are you talking about?"

She lowered her trembling hand, her other gripping her cell phone so hard her fingers started to cramp. Yes, she'd willingly married Clayton. Willingly stayed with him, too. And she had cared for him. Deeply. But the truth—a truth Clayton probably understood even more than April, at that point—was that she really had agreed to the arrangement solely out of gratitude. And that, had she known then what she knew now, she wasn't sure she'd make the same choice.

"I married Clayton as a favor," she finally said. "Or I should say, to repay him for his."

Even over the phone, she could sense her mother going very still. "I thought... I'm sorry, honey, I don't understand. Are you saying it was a marriage of convenience?"

"Yes."

A long silence preceded, "For whom?"

"Both of us."

"Because..." Her mother sucked in a sharp breath. "Because of everything he did for us when your father was so ill."

"Partly. And we *were* friends. But only friends." She paused. "It never struck you as odd that Clay was so much older? That we weren't, um, exactly on the same social level?"

"Oh, please. Rich, older men take trophy wives all the time. And you were—still are—a knockout. And as long as you were happy...oh, dear God. Were you?"

"He was good to me. To the best of his ability."

"Meaning...?"

"He was sick when I married him," she said quietly, deciding not to get into the other, especially since she had no proof. Nor was his sexual preference germane, when all was said and done. "That was my favor to him, as a gift to his mother. But Clay was a sweet, kind, very generous man, and I obviously benefitted far more than I could have ever imagined. Although I truly didn't marry him for his money. Not for me, I mean. But…" She sighed. "But I knew if I did he'd make sure you and Daddy were taken care of."

It didn't dawn on April until much later that in all likelihood Clay would have seen to her parents' well-being anyway, even if she'd refused his proposal, simply because his heart was that big. As was his bank account. That the sense of obligation had been entirely in her head, not his. But at twenty-one, she didn't know that. Didn't know him. More to the point, she didn't know who *she* was, or what she really needed. And once she'd made that promise…

"I had no idea, honey," Mama said. "I really didn't."

"I know. And I'm sorry for keeping you in the dark, but it seemed best. At least at the time."

"And now…" Her mother spoke slowly, as though a few things were beginning to make sense. "And now you're finally doing something for yourself."

Even though she knew Mama was talking about the inn, April was glad her mother couldn't see her blush as the image of Patrick's want-you-now gaze shimmered in her head, as she suddenly craved his touch, wanted to touch *him,* so badly her womb cramped.

"It's about time, don't you think?" she said, calling out, "Yes?" to the knock on the door.

Todd poked his head inside. "The Eddlestons are here. If you're busy I can take care of them—"

"No, no, I'll be right there." Then, to her mother, "Guests are here, I need to go. I guess we'll talk later?"

"Absolutely," Mama said, sounding subdued. And still a little floored. "April?"

"Yes?"

"I love you, baby. You know that, right?"

Her eyes swam. "Of course I do. I love you, too."

But as she hung up, she wondered…was she still denying herself? That for all she was grateful for what she did have with Patrick, for all she understood and respected his need to be cautious, did at least part of her impatience, or annoyance, or whatever it was stem from her once again accepting an okay-for-now relationship as, well, okay?

Definitely something to ponder.

Smiling, she greeted the Eddlestons, a pair of no-nonsense retirees from Baltimore whom April immediately pegged as birders, with their sensible shoes and camera/binocular cases hanging around their necks. Signed them in. Swiped their credit card. Gave them keys to their room.

Realized, as she led them upstairs, that Patrick wasn't the only one holding back. Only what if by giving Patrick whatever emotional space he seemed to need, she was unwittingly sending the message that she wasn't entirely willing to move forward, either? That she really was fine with a fling?

It was all so confusing, she thought as she ushered the couple into the corner bedroom with an en suite bath, done in Blythe's signature eclectic style in tans and rich reds, with the occasional purple "pop." When did *committed* cross the line to *suffocating?* How was she supposed to let Patrick know she wasn't going anywhere without making the poor guy feel trapped?

"Oh, isn't this lovely!" Mrs. Eddleston said, setting down her camera case on the antique writing desk before plodding to the window to take in the river view, the water gone a deep crimson in the setting sun.

"Thank you."

"And this is your own house?"

"Now, yes. It had been my grandmother's. My cousins and I spent our summers here, when we were children."

"And you loved it," Mrs. Eddleston gently said.

"I did."

"I can tell." The white-haired woman turned back to April, her wrinkled face aglow from the sun—and something that clearly came from within. "Did I see something on your website, that you host weddings, too?"

"We haven't actually done one yet, but we plan to." April grinned, even as her heart twinged. "Thinking about renewing your vows?"

Chuckling, the older woman poked her husband, who'd come to stand beside her, squinting like Mr. Magoo as he cleaned his glasses. "Wouldn't this be perfect for Lisa's wedding?" When he grunted, his wife gave him an indulgent look, then said to April, "Our granddaughter. Her boyfriend's planning to ask her to marry him at Christmas, although she doesn't know it." She chuckled. "We're not supposed to, either, I suspect, but her mother is so excited she couldn't keep it to herself."

And if April was going to get all *verklempt* every time somebody got married under that gazebo she was screwed. "I have brochures about our wedding services, if you'd like to take some home with you—"

"Oh, that would be perfect, dear! Thank you!"

"I'll let you settle in then," April said, smiling as Mr. Eddleston made a beeline for one of the two wing chairs facing the flat-screen TV, hovering over the fireplace across from the canopied bed. "The dining room opens at five-thirty, you'll find tonight's menu on the desk. If there's anything you need, don't hesitate to ask. And we're very informal, no need to dress up!"

She left the couple to it, smacking aside her cloudy mood as she trooped back downstairs to check on Mel and her new assistant, Sylvia, in the kitchen.

The whole downstairs smelled of herbed roast chicken and grilled vegetables and seafood stew, chocolate and browned butter and fresh baked rolls. For now, the restaurant was only open five nights a week, although the plan was to quickly move to seven, since by the end of their first week of business, the tiny dining room had been filled most of the evening. Mel had been beside herself with glee. As had April, needless to say.

"Hey, Sylvia! How's it going?"

A shy smile preceded, "Fine, Ms. Ross. And you?"

After weeks of interviewing and bemoaning the lack of decent candidates, Mel finally found someone she felt she could train to her exacting standards, the granddaughter of an old farmer Mel's mother would take them all to visit from time to time during those childhood summers. Tall, thin and almost eerily focused, the pretty young woman chopped salad veggies at the island work station, her long, chocolate-brown dreads tied back with what looked like cooking string…a modest engagement diamond winking on her left ring finger.

Then April turned to Mel, and wouldn't you know her eyes went right to Mel's pink diamond ring, as well, and April's own finger itched, the groove not yet filled in, and she practically rolled her eyes at herself for being a dingdong.

"Try the sauce for the chicken, see what you think," Mel said as she disappeared into the pantry, a room nearly as big as the guest bedrooms.

April took a spoon from the drawer, tasted. Pulled her eyes back into her head. "Fabulous—"

"Damn," came from the pantry. "Hey, Sylvia—didn't Anderson's deliver more olive oil today?"

"Yesterday. But I thought we had an extra can, anyway." The girl left the table to join Mel in the pantry. April heard rummaging, some mild cussing. She took another taste of the sauce. Shivered.

"I did, too," Mel said. "I must've used more than I realized."

"You want me to run into town and get more?" Sylvia offered.

"But then I don't have you here—"

"I'll do it," April said, tearing herself away from the sauce. "The Eddlestons look pretty settled for a while, and Todd can take care of things for a half hour. Tell me exactly what you need."

Which is how it came to pass that, fifteen minutes later, April pulled up in front of St. Mary's only reasonably sized food market to find Patrick squatting off to the side by the front door, doing his best to console a sobbing four-year-old in a complete meltdown.

Chapter Ten

"Anything I can do?"

Barely able to hear over Lili's wails, Patrick's head shot up, his heart knocking when he saw April. And if it was wrong to be glad to see her—to see anybody who wasn't giving him dirty and/or pitying looks right now—then, tough.

Until he realized her words didn't exactly match the what-do-I-do-now? expression on her face.

Shaking his head, he pushed himself to his feet, hauling his sobbing daughter into his arms and cupping her head to his shoulder as she howled. He just kept hugging and shushing, hugging and shushing, occasionally catching April still standing there, her face all scrunched up like she really did want to make it better, even if she didn't know how. But not like Lili's display particularly bothered her. Then some old biddy Patrick didn't know must've said something April took offense to—he couldn't exactly hear, but he got the gist—because she swung around and said something back and the biddy scurried off.

Then, without further ado, she pried Lili out of his arms, went over to a nearby bench and sat down with her, stroking her hair and singing to her or something. *Yeah, good luck with that,* he wanted to say, except damned if the wails didn't get softer, until after a couple seconds Lili slumped against April's chest, stuck her thumb in her mouth and basically passed out.

Ripped him right in two. Even more than he'd been before.

Blowing out a breath, Patrick sank onto the bench beside them, his thoughts jumbled up yet again, that it should be Natalie holding Lili. Except it wasn't, it was April. Crazy, fearless April who wasn't about to let a little thing like not knowing what the hell she was doing stop her from *trying,* and if Patrick didn't know better he might think he'd fallen for her.

Oh, hell, *no,* he thought even as he said, "How'd you do that?"

"I have no idea," April whispered. "And I didn't mean to overstep, I swear, but it occurred to me maybe she was picking up on your tension."

She shifted the toddler to lay her head on Lili's curls, those big turquoise eyes boring right into his, and everything inside him ached. Like, you know, he wanted to keep her.

"What happened?" she asked.

"Darned if I know…no, wait. When I got her out of her car seat, she took off and I had to run after her. Scared the sh—uh, crud out of me. I might've come on a little strong when I said 'no' since she gave me this really strange look. But she didn't lose it until we got into a tussle about her sitting in the cart."

April chuckled, both easing the knot and tightening it more, which made no sense whatsoever. "Little Miss Independent?" she said.

"You can say that again. You really weren't bothered? By her, um, display?"

Another chuckle preceded, "After living with my mother-in-law, trust me, an occasionally crabby four-year-old holds no terror."

Lili jerked awake, tilted her head back to give April a confused look, then lunged for Patrick. He grabbed her, getting a whiff of April as he did, stirring up all manner of thoughts highly inappropriate to the occasion. Especially when he noticed her arms clamped across her middle, like something had been ripped away from her, as well as the slight hurt in her eyes when Lili snuggled up to him and once more conked out.

"Thanks," he said, wondering if the world would implode if he leaned over and kissed her. Or he would, if he didn't. It'd been two days since their last encounter, since he'd heard her laugh, felt her smile heat him through. Two days of walking around feeling like he was constantly hungry. "Guess you came along at the right time."

"Guess so," she said, hooking her purse over her shoulder as she stood, and the thought of them going their separate ways, like this was only some chance encounter between acquaintances, suddenly annoyed him no end—

Own it, bonehead.

Whatever this is between you, own *it.*

His head spinning, he got to his feet as well, Lili heavy in his arms. An elderly couple came out of the store, the woman giving Lili a little "Aw, isn't she an angel?" before they moved on to their car. The knot eased up some. Then he noticed April's funny little smile.

"How are you going to do your shopping?"

"I'll just pick up what I most need for now, come back later—"

"I don't know what to do here," she said softly, and Patrick's stomach jumped.

"What?"

A breeze ruffled her hair; she tugged off her tortoiseshell headband, shoved it back into place. "I'd like to invite you and Lili back to the inn for dinner, except I'm afraid you'd feel threatened, that I was being too pushy. I mean, I understand your concern about Lili, I do—I'd probably be the same way if she were mine. But…" She hauled in a breath. "But I also can't help feeling you're…you're using her as a reason to hold yourself back, so you don't have to explore what's going on between us."

Annoyance heated his skin, even as his brother-in-law's words echoed underneath his skull. "And that's a crock."

"Is it?" she said gently, giving him one of those steady looks that both turned him on and made him antsy as all hell.

Patrick half wanted to bolt, half wanted to give in to the pull, to let himself feed off all that sweet strength until he was sated. If that were even possible.

He waited until a woman with two kids passed and went into the store. "I thought we agreed this was only between us."

"How is that even possible? Lili's not only a huge part of your life, she's part of who you are. And my heart…" Her lips barely curved, she looked at Lili, then back at him. "There's a lot of room in there, Patrick. A *lot* of room. And the thing is, I've already been in one limited relationship, even if the parameters were diametrically opposite of this one. Yes, I know…by my choice. But what can I say? My concept of 'it'll do' has expanded."

"Meaning you've decided to change the rules."

"Meaning I was wrong to accept those rules to begin with. Then again, I wasn't exactly thinking clearly at that point," she said with a smirk which immediately shifted to a frown as she laid her hand on his arm. "As much as I'm enjoying what we have, I know that ultimately it's not going to be enough. I want more, Patrick. I *deserve* more. Or at least I deserve the opportunity to see if there could be more. And you know what?"

She leaned toward him and whispered, "So do you. You and that precious little girl, both," before turning to go into the store.

His breathing ragged, Patrick shifted Lili in his arms and stalked back to his truck, deciding he'd rather pay the jacked-up prices for milk and bread at the 7-Eleven than risk running into April again in the supermarket. Dammit, where did she get off saying this stuff? She didn't know him, didn't know Lili, and for damn sure didn't know what either of them needed, or deserved. Or even wanted, when it came right down to it. Only, once he got his sacked-out kid in her seat and himself behind the wheel, it felt like somebody slapped the back of his head.

He glanced at his daughter, a tiny frown etched in her brow as she slept, then faced front again, doing some heavy-duty frowning of his own.

Own it?

At this point, he didn't even know how to borrow it.

"What took you so long?" Mel barked, snatching the can of oil out of April's hands when she walked in, yanking off the lid and pouring some into a cast-iron pan on the stove. April exchanged a glance with Sylvia, who gave a little shrug and went back to artistically arranging things on plates.

"I ran into Patrick. And Lili." April plunked her purse

at the far end of the counter and snitched a parboiled mini carrot slated for candying from the bowl beside the stove. "Poor kid was in a heap by the store's front door, sobbing her heart out." When she went for another carrot, Mel lightly smacked the top of her hand with a wooden spoon.

"Yeah, Quinn was the mistress of losing it in public. Love the way people look at you like 'Why are you beating your kid?' Or, better, 'Why *aren't* you beating that kid?'" She added a good chunk of butter to the oil, dumped the carrots into the sizzling mixture. "So what happened?"

Good question. "I took her from Patrick, then sat with her until she calmed down. Like I knew what I was doing and everything."

"Yeah?"

"Yeah. Well, until Lili realized I wasn't her daddy and practically broke something trying to get back to him."

Mel chuckled. "Don't take it personally, hon. Kids aren't known for their diplomatic skills."

"I know, but…" April clamped shut her mouth.

That got a narrowed gaze. "Keep going."

Although April still wasn't dispensing details, her sleeping with Patrick wasn't exactly a secret. Even so, she waited until Sylvia left to use the bathroom before sharing her recent revelation—and her half-baked dinner invitation—with her cousin. "Although I doubt he even remembers it," she sighed out. "Besides, I really should have asked you first—"

"Are you kidding? We could probably feed his entire Shaughnessy clan with the leftovers alone. No, that was good. Tossing the ball in his court."

"Which he handily dodged." Another sigh. "Probably because I'm acting like some stalking teenybopper."

"More like a woman with the stones to tell a man what she really wants." Stirring, Mel gave her a thumbs-up.

"Only now I've scared him away."

"I doubt it," Mel said, spooning in some brown sugar and a generous drizzle of balsamic vinegar. "Then again, men are weird. They *say* they want us to be up-front so they don't have to guess what we're thinking. But when we are, they get all bent out of shape. They also get over it. Usually."

"Gee, thanks."

Mel gave April's arm a quick squeeze, then turned off the flame under the carrots, moving the pan from the burner. "Um…Ry and I set a date, by the way."

Dragging herself away from her pity party, April grinned. "Oh, yeah? When?"

"Early June. Right there in the gazebo. If that's okay with you?"

"Of course! But not at his parents' house?"

Mel gave April a look. "Yeah, right."

"I thought you said you were past all that."

"I am." Her mouth flattened. "Okay, his folks and I are working on it. But I'd rather get married here, anyway. You think Aunt Tilda and Uncle Ed would come?"

"Oh, gosh, who knows?" she said as Mel went to the main sink to wash her hands. "Although I suppose miracles do happen."

But honestly…did human beings have a hard time with letting go of the past, or what?

"Well, would you lookee there?" Mel said softly, peering outside.

"What?" April joined her, only to gasp when she saw Patrick and an unusually subdued Lili, her hand fast in his as they made their way toward the back entrance. He glanced up, giving a little wave when he saw April in the window.

"Holy cannoli, girl." Chuckling, Mel elbowed April in the arm. "You *rule*."

Not hardly, she thought as she met them at the back door, smiling for the obviously skeptical Lili before lifting her gaze to the child's equally skeptical father.

Hiking Lili into his arms, his eyes caressed hers, fear warring with obvious longing as something like a smile pulled at his mouth. "Okay. Let's try this your way."

A huge step for him, she knew. Even if one with no guarantees.

"Deal," she said, welcoming them inside.

On her knees in front of a box of ornaments hauled from Frannie's house, April slid her gaze to Patrick where he sat on his sofa gamely trying to untangle a wad of lights...in between casting worried glances in his child's direction. Beside April, said child rummaged through said box, occasionally holding up one for April to admire and breaking her heart in the process. Because a week later, April had learned three things: 1) she loved Lilianna with all her heart; 2) she loved the little girl's daddy even more; and 3) managing an inn was a walk in the park compared with breaking the pair of them out of their emotional prison.

And with each day she found herself more and more tempted to believe she wasn't up to the job.

In the corner, a small, fragrant fir patiently waited to be dressed, while Christmas carols played softly from April's docked iPod. The perfect family holiday scenario, right? Except for the trying-too-hard tension throbbing beneath the surface that, while it occasionally eased enough to be almost imperceptible, also had a nasty habit of suddenly and without warning yanking taut, throwing them all off balance.

It's only been a week. Patience, girl. Patience.

Lili's sparkling laugh cut through her thoughts. "Look, April," she said, holding up a cross-eyed Santa all tangled up in a pair of skis. "He's funny."

"He certainly is," she said, thinking it was moments like this—sometimes as brief as a heartbeat—that gave her hope that she and Lili might hit it off, after all. That the child's father might someday actually be able to stop holding his breath.

April, too.

It didn't help that today, as they'd lined up on Main Street for the parade that kicked off St. Mary's ten-day Christmas festival, Lili's mother had called on Patrick's phone. The call had barely lasted five minutes, just long enough to put the child in a bad mood that no amount of hot chocolate with whipped cream or gingerbread men could assuage, a bad mood that had followed them all day like a stinky cloud. Until now.

Who knew all it would take to break through the fog was a silly Santa with sketchy alpine skills? Emboldened, April gave Lili a quick, one-armed hug, which at least earned her a smile…before the child deliberately scooted away. *Don't take it personally,* Mel had said, words April had probably repeated to herself a hundred times over the past week. And would keep repeating as long as it took.

"Hey." Determined to reinforce what she'd been trying to show him all week, that Lili's mood swings weren't about to derail how she felt about either of them, April grinned over at Patrick. "You with the lights. Planning on having them strung before New Year's?"

"Yeah, Daddy," Lili added, her little forehead all scrunched up. "April says we can't put on any of the orda-mints until the lights are on. So snap to it, huh?"

And with that, the pall dispersed. Or at least April wanted to believe it had as she swallowed down her laugh.

Even Patrick's mouth twitched, his gaze meeting hers. A gaze unfortunately as ambivalent as ever. But again, it'd only been a week.

"Yes, ma'am," he said to Lili as he stood, plugged in the lights and started to wind them around the tree, and April released a tiny bit more of that breath, thinking, *Pearls*. Not the ones she'd cast, she thought with a smile, but the ones she and Patrick were gathering together, these cherished moments of peace. Of rightness. Now she could only pray the string holding them didn't break....

The colored lights reminded Patrick of when he was a kid, since that's what they always had. Still did, on the "big" tree taking up half his parents' living room—

He was trying. Trying to make a home for his child, to make her childhood as secure as his had been. Trying to give April and him a chance at that "more," even though he felt like he was stumbling around as blindly with that as he was with the father thing. And heaven knew he was trying to be patient, to be open, with her, with Lili...with himself.

Behind him, he heard Lili's chatter as she pawed through the ornaments, April's gentle responses as she let the kid steer the conversation. The three of them had spent as much time together as possible this past week, and not once had he seen her lose her cool, or react to one of Lili's fits. It wasn't like he'd never seen her get irked—with him, with her cousins, or when something went awry at the inn. She was human. But never with his little girl. If anything, he'd seen nothing but compassion on her face...for both of them. A compassion that wasn't faked, but simply part of who she was. An example that made Patrick remember who *he* was, what he believed in. What, despite the fear still lodged in his chest, he still wanted.

Which was, he'd finally admitted to himself, to believe

in forever like she did. And that, somehow, he might absorb April's confidence and optimism. So he could, you know, be what she needed. Be her hero, like he wanted to be Lili's. Because otherwise she'd be shouldering the entire load, and no way in hell would he do that to her.

So, yeah. He was trying, he thought as April left to go make hot chocolate in the closed-off kitchen. Trying to push through this last barrier keeping him from normal, to accept the good right in front of him, even if he couldn't see further into the future than the end of his nose…or hadn't yet entirely shaken off the past, still gripping his ankles, if not his throat—

"Can I help?"

His chest ached as he grinned down at Lili. "Tell you what—why don't you hold out the string for me so it doesn't get all tangled again. Just make sure to hang on to it between the lights, they might be hot."

"'Kay." The little girl grabbed the string, dangling it way over her head so that insanely kissable pot belly pooched out from underneath her red sweater. "I really, really like Christmas," she said on a languid sigh, making Patrick send up a little prayer of gratitude. Maybe they'd get through this holiday, after all, even if Natalie still wouldn't commit to seeing her own kid at Christmas.

"I bet you do."

"Do *you*?"

"Sure," he said, because this wasn't about him. Not that he had anything against holidays, but he sure wouldn't be scratching the hell out of himself stringing lights on this blasted tree if it weren't for his kid. And God knows he wouldn't have nearly frozen his butt nailing evergreen swags across way too many feet of porch overhang at the inn if it hadn't been for April. Who was apparently every bit as wide-eyed about Christmas as his preschooler.

He tugged at the string, making Lili drop it. With another sigh, she bent over and picked up the next length, her forehead puckered again as one blue light apparently sucked her in.

"Will Santa bring me presents?"

"I'm sure he will."

She was quiet for a long time, then asked, "Would he bring me Mama if I asked?"

Patrick's stomach fell. It was like hearing those first, faint thunder rumbles that signaled a storm was about to hit.

"I think that's between Santa and Mama, baby," he said carefully.

"Could *you* ask her to come?"

"I could," he said, even more carefully. "But I can't *make* her come."

"Why not?"

"Because people can't make other people do things. Just the way it works."

"You make me brush my teeth. An' go to bed when I don't wanna."

Hell. That string done, Patrick grabbed the second one off the floor to plug it into the first. "That's different, baby," he said, handing Lili the end. "That's taking care of you, not ordering you around."

Her nose wrinkled. "You sure?"

"Yeah. I'm sure."

She started swinging the string like a jump rope, making the little lights bang against Patrick's leg. "The colors are all swirly," she said, giggling, and Patrick whooshed out a breath, that maybe they'd gotten over that hurdle. Until she said, "How come I never go to Mama's house?" and he realized, *Nope*.

"You'd have to ask Mama that."

"I did. On the phone. She wouldn't t-tell me." At the catch in Lili's voice, he looked over to see a tear dribble down her soft cheek. She crouched, stretching the string across her knees. "Why did she go away, anyway?" she said softly. "Did I do something bad?"

The lights clattered when Patrick dropped them to squat in front of his little girl, hardly even reacting when she reached up to run her fingers over the ruched skin on his cheek, something he'd finally realized some months ago she did to soothe herself.

"No, baby, of course you didn't do anything bad."

"Then why does she hardly *ever* come? Or let me go to her house?"

Holy hell—where was all this coming from? She'd never asked questions like this before. Was it because she didn't have the words before now? Or because April being around was stirring them up?

And once again, was it right letting Lili get close to somebody else before she had any of this about her mother sorted out in her head?

He released a breath. "Honey, I don't know why your mama does half the things she does. Maybe she doesn't want you to see her house because, I don't know, it's messy or something. Because she's been too busy to clean it."

Lili looked around the cluttered living room, then back at him, frowning. "But I like messy houses."

And wouldn't his mother croak if she heard that? "I'm sorry, baby, I wish I could answer for Mama, tell you what she's thinking. But I can't. I know she loves you, though."

His chest cramped when tears flooded Lili's dark brown eyes. "Then why doesn't she want to see me? Why d-does she only stay for a m-minute an' then go away again?"

He pulled Lili into his arms, his own eyes stinging as he whispered, "I don't know, baby, I don't know."

He heard April return from the kitchen, his old beat-up serving tray softly thunking onto the battle-scarred coffee table when she set it down. Wordlessly, she picked up the abandoned light string and started tucking it into the tree, and the weird thing was Patrick couldn't decide if he was glad she was there or wished she wasn't. And between that and not having a clue what to say to his daughter, he could see the panic attack lurking right outside his vision, snarling and snapping and pacing, trying to find a way in. His eyes shut, he held on to his little girl, breathing deeply and steadily like the therapist had taught him, until the damn thing slunk away.

For now. But for those couple moments when it felt like he was going to lose control…

Not an option. Especially not now. And whatever he had to do to relieve the pressure, he would.

"Lights are done," April said softly, and Patrick felt sick inside. "Lili, you want to pick the first ornament to hang on the tree?"

She nodded against his chest, then pulled away, wiping her nose on her sleeve. Chuckling, April handed her a tissue, holding it to her nose to help her blow. Acting like everything was fine when it was perfectly obvious it wasn't. She wasn't stupid, she had to know.

The crazy Santa hung, Lili announced she had to pee and ran down the short hall to the bathroom.

And Patrick collapsed into the armchair next to the tree, leaning forward with his head in his hands.

Some hero, he thought.

Some *freaking* hero.

"Here," April said, holding a cup of hot chocolate in front of Patrick, even as hope shriveled inside her. Because in the ten minutes it had taken to make the cocoa, the tension had not only pulled taut, it had completely snapped. "Cocoa cures everything. I promise."

After a moment he lifted his head, one side of his mouth slightly pulled up. "Thanks." He took the mug, licking the whipped cream off his upper lip after his first sip. "How much did you hear?"

"Enough."

Enough for it to finally penetrate that parades and trimming trees and hot chocolate weren't going to magically fix things. That *April* wasn't going to magically fix things. And that as much as Lili had already wrapped her curly headed self around her heart, April couldn't be the one thing the little girl most wanted: her own mother. At least at the moment. True, maybe with enough love and patience, things could work out in the future. But if Lili and Patrick—especially Patrick—were clearly too firmly rooted in the present to trust that, to trust *her*...well.

None of Patrick's other objections, she now realized, meant squat. Not his questioning her motives about why she'd picked him, not her sexual inexperience, not his leftover hurt about his ex-wife's abandonment. Or even what she suspected were lingering self-confidence issues stemming from his appearance, although she would have thought those, especially, had been shoved *way* behind them. What was going on with his daughter, though, was bigger than all the rest combined. Far bigger.

And completely outside her control.

April sat on the sturdy old coffee table, her hands gripping the edge on either side of her hips, feeling her pulse throb in her temples. She'd—they'd—had such lovely plans for tonight, including her staying over, testing the waters of what life might be like in the future. Patrick's suggestion, she thought as her throat clogged.

His eyes fixed straight ahead, he took another swallow of his drink, then sagged back into the chair, the mug propped on one worn arm as he scrubbed the heel of his hand into his eye, his obvious exhaustion breaking her heart.

"Part of me thinks," he said as his hand banged down on the other chair arm, "if I could get through to Nat what she was doing to Lili, maybe we could fix this. Only then I think, what good would it do? Because Lili doesn't want explanations, she wants her mother. And that's the one thing I can't give her. God—I *hate* feeling so damn *useless*."

A frustration only the strong experienced, April suspected. She frowned anyway. "You really think that? At least you're *here* for her. I imagine a lot of men in your... in your situation would have handed the kid off to a relative and said, *Forget this*. But you didn't."

"No," he said after a moment, then lifted harrowed eyes to hers. "Doesn't mean I haven't thought about it from time to time. If it wouldn't be better for her if I gave custody to one of my brothers or sisters. You know, somebody who knew what they were doing?"

Unable to bear his pained expression, April twisted around to get her own mug of cocoa, lifting it to her lips with a smile. "I take it that leaves Luke out of the running, then?"

That actually got a little laugh. "True."

After a moment's thought, she set down her mug and crossed to the chair, questions flickering across his features a second before she leaned over, took his face in her hands and kissed him. None too gently, either. "And do you have any idea," she said when she was done, a breath away from his mouth, "how much courage it takes to admit that?"

He covered her hand with his, his fingers bumping over her knuckles and a gentle smile curving his lips, even as apology swam in his eyes. "This habit you have of always seeing the good in people? Really annoying."

She forced herself to smile back. "So I've been told," she said, straightening when she heard the bathroom door bang open, followed by Lili charging down the hall.

"Did you wash your hands?" Patrick asked.

"Uh-huh. See?" She held them out. Presumably to show they were still wet. Then they resumed trimming the tree, as though everything was hunky-dory when everyone in the room knew it wasn't. April could only guess what was going through Patrick's head, although his seeming reluctance to look at her for more than a second or two—when before he'd had no problem telegraphing exactly what he was thinking—told her everything she needed to know.

At last the tree was done, a bright spot of magic in the cramped little room, and, after a few minutes of well-earned tree worship, Patrick whisked away a protesting Lili to put her to bed. Her chest tight, April washed the mugs and set them in the drainer, then returned to the living room to straighten up the empty ornament boxes, collect a dozen scattered toys and return them to the wicker basket on the bookshelf beside the TV. A nice room, she thought, the mishmash of cast-offs and hand-me-downs somehow coalescing into something warm and appealing, despite the generic off-white walls and plain beige carpet remnant covering most of the worn wood floors.

And Lili was everywhere, from the plastic art easel set up in one corner to dozens of paintings and drawings tacked up on one wall, to a bright red beanbag dog taking up most of another corner, to the slew of Dr. Seuss hardbacks scattered across the coffee table, all of it shouting, *This is my life.*

First and foremost, this is who I am.

Her hands like ice, April stacked the books, gathered

her coat and purse, then sat on the edge of the same chair Patrick had been in earlier. The tree's colored lights looked like melted gumdrops through her flooded eyes as she waited for him, fighting the urge to run.

But that would be rude. And very un-her. So she stayed, feeling her stomach turn inside out when she heard his footsteps coming down the hall. Seeing her with her purse and jacket, his brows crashed.

"You're leaving?"

As she stood, a light snow began to tick against the windows. Heaven knew she'd given this thing her all. As had Patrick, more than either of them had probably thought possible a month ago. And the idea of giving up, of giving up on *him,* made her ill. Then again, she could still change her mind, couldn't she? What was preventing her from dropping her things, taking his hand and leading him to his bedroom?

Then she felt it, like a hand on her shoulder, heard a voice whisper, *"Let go."*

She'd only wanted to bring him joy, not more stress. And she'd like to think she had, even if only for a while. But if the timing wasn't right, it wasn't right, and all the wishing in the world wasn't going to change that. "I never meant to make things worse, Patrick. For either of you."

"Damn, April—"

"So I think it's best. That I leave."

After a moment, he closed the space between them to pull her tight against his chest, rubbing his cheek in her hair. When she felt him swallow, she shut her eyes, still wishing…hoping….

"I'm so sorry," he whispered. "So, so sorry. But please…" He took her face in his hands, ducking to meet her gaze, his own so tortured it tore her in two. "It's not your fault."

He'd never said he loved her. In fact he'd gone out of his way not to lead her on or fuel her dreams. Yet her hands fisted against the breath-stealing pain—no less excruciating because she'd known the blow was coming. How her heart was even still beating, she did not know. Or maybe it wasn't, it was hard to tell, what with feeling like all the air had been crushed right out of her.

"I'm sorry, too," she said, and he kissed her, killing her a little more before she pulled away, gathered her things and left. Miraculously she held it together while she drove, so she wouldn't start bawling and drive off the road and get herself killed, no matter how much she didn't much care right then if she lived or not.

And yes, she thought when she got back to the inn, sneaking in through her private entrance so she wouldn't run into anybody, she was acting like a melodramatic fifteen-year-old. Since she'd never had a reason or the opportunity to act like a melodramatic fifteen-year-old when she *was* fifteen, she figured she was overdue. As long as nobody saw her, what difference did it make?

The light knock on the door to her den made her jump.

"April?" Mel said. "Come on, I know you're home, I saw you pull in as I was walking out to my car."

And of course she hadn't *kept* walking.

"I thought you were spending the night at Patrick's? Is everything okay?"

April opened her mouth to say *Of course it is, why wouldn't it be?* except nothing came out except this hideous sound, like a wounded moose.

"That's it, I'm coming in…"

Two seconds later she was wrapped in her cousin's arms, blubbering for all she was worth.

Chapter Eleven

As the late December night swallowed up the dusk, Patrick stood at the end of the marina, Lili's hand firmly grasped in his as dozens of brightly lit boats chugged past in the nautical parade, another St. Mary's tradition going back twenty years or so and drawing more of a crowd every year.

Three days before Christmas. A week since April walked out of his apartment.

A week since he'd *let* her walk out, telling himself it was for the best, he should have never dragged her into this mess he called a life, anyway. That there simply wasn't enough of him to go around.

And yet, when he'd spotted her and Mel at their booth in the town square earlier, heard her laugh long before he saw her, he'd felt sliced in two. When Nat had left them, there'd been pain, sure—of failure, of rejection. But to be honest there'd also been relief, that he'd no longer have to see the disappointment on her face, or feel the frustration that came from trying to revive something long dead. With April, though, there was just pain.

Like being ripped apart from the inside.

"Wondered where you're gotten to," his mother said as she squeezed in beside him to link her arm through his. He'd said little to his family other than it hadn't worked out between him and April, and amazingly enough, they'd all kept their traps shut. Except for Luke, who'd suggested they go get wasted—apparently he was having woman troubles, as well—and Neil and Frannie had doled out nearly identical "You're an idiot" looks that had almost made him laugh.

But other than giving him a hug, his mother had remained silent. Until now, he suspected. He also figured that, as with some of the more gruesome remedies she'd inflicted on them when they were kids, the sooner he let her do what she was gonna do, the sooner it would be over and he could go back to suffering in peace.

"Right here, Mrs. Claus," he said, and she chuckled. His father had been playing town Santa for as long as Patrick could remember. Even had a special pair of wire-rimmed glasses so the kids wouldn't recognize him. Made a damn good one, too, perched on his gold-and-velvet throne in a heated, over-decorated tent in the square. He'd even tricked Lili tonight, Patrick thought, his gut knotting as he remembered that shared glance with his father when Lili really did ask him to bring her mother back.

"Saw April earlier," Ma said, softly enough that Lili wouldn't hear. "She looks more miserable that you do."

And here it comes. "I saw her, too. She looked fine to me."

"Then I'm guessing you didn't see her up close."

He pulled in a breath. It didn't help. "She broke it off, Ma—"

"Hey, Lili!" They turned to see his sister Frannie, practically swallowed up in a wooly hat and long scarf. "One of Uncle Neil's buddies said we could go out on his boat to see the lights better! Wanna come?"

Lili spun around to Patrick, eyes huge, an irresistible grin lighting up her whole face. "Can I?"

For tonight, she'd been happy, perhaps because she'd finally been able to put in her request to Santa. If she missed April, she hadn't said. And no way was Patrick going to bring up the subject.

"Oh, I suppose," he said with an exaggerated sigh guaranteed to make her giggle. "But make sure she's wearing a life jacket!" he yelled to his sister as the kid bolted away like a rabbit with a coyote on her tail. Laughing, Frannie grabbed Lili's hand, yelling back they'd take her home with them when they were done, to pick her up later.

Patrick turned back to the water, leaning his forearms against the railing bordering the end of the dock. "And I smell a setup."

His mother smiled. "I prefer to think of it as God working out His purpose through us."

Yeah, she would think that. "It would have ended, anyway. Between April and me."

"Since you'd already predetermined the outcome, you mean?" When he tensed, she patted his arm and said, "I've watched you guys nurse a lot of heartbreaks over the years. Relationships don't always work out, I get it. And sometimes, they shouldn't. I get that, too. But I also know that when a breakup leaves both parties as unhappy as you and April seem to be, then something's not right."

"Ma—"

"Look, simply because Natalie left you high and dry doesn't mean every woman will—"

"But April *did* leave."

"And what did you do to stop her?"

"What makes you think there's anything I could have done? Look, Lili's going through all this crap about her mother, it just seemed best to call it off now. Before anyone got hurt."

"Before you let yourself need her too much, you mean."

His stomach clenched. "And you're overstepping."

"We've already established that. And unless you push me into the drink I'm going to continue to overstep because I love you. You deserve someone special in your life, sweetheart. You and Lili, both—"

"We've got you guys. We're fine."

"And you can't keep leeching off of us forever, you know."

Patrick jerked his head down so fast his neck popped. "Is that what you think I'm doing?"

"Actually, yes. I do. Because we're safe, and we're here, and it's easy. And of course we'll always *be* here for you and Lili. But honestly, Patrick—here this lovely, lov*ing* woman comes along, someone who clearly adores Lili *and* can put up with your chronic grumpiness, and you didn't even think to fight for her? And don't you shake your head at me, young man. I saw how you looked at April when you were over for dinner last week. More importantly, how she looked at *you*. And heaven knows I never saw Natalie look at you like that—"

"Ma. Please. Let it go, okay?"

He got maybe five, six seconds of peace before his mother withdrew her arm to rub his back. "You're one of the bravest, most generous people I know, my love. But you're also one of the most mule headed. And thank God for it, or there'd be a couple men who wouldn't be alive right now. In fact, I can't recall you ever backing down from a challenge, or giving up on something simply because there was a chance it wouldn't work out." She paused. "Or that you might get hurt. So how is this any different?"

Irritation heated his face. "How about, because someone else's happiness is at stake here? Lili's *and* April's."

"And your own?"

He looked away. "That's not important."

"Don't be ridiculous, of course it is. Because Lili's never going to heal until you do. What kind of example are you setting for her if you keep closing yourself off?"

Her cell phone buzzed. She dug it out of her coat pocket, extending it slightly to read the text. "Ah. Your father. Wondering where I am." After texting him back, she slipped the phone into her pocket again and said, "You know, giving is all well and good, but the concept doesn't work without someone to receive the blessing on the other end." Palms up, she imitated a scale coming into balance. "Yin/yang and all that. Otherwise the giving goes to waste, doesn't it?"

With that she pulled him down for a hug, then wove back through the crowd to find his father.

Thinking a triple dose of cod liver oil would have been preferable to that conversation, Patrick gave up his prime spot to another dad and his kids, then wandered back off the pier and toward the square, feeling adrift as he wended his way through the irritatingly jolly crowds. All of Main Street sparkled, ancient tinsel wreaths adorning the streetlamps like so many spunky old chorus girls brought out of retirement every year. Anchoring one corner of the square was his old parish church, that great-aunt in her conservative brown tweeds quietly reminding everyone what the fuss was really about. Should be, anyway. A weathered, life-size nativity scene graced the winter-withered lawn on one side of the church steps; above them, a warm glow beckoned from the open center doors, inviting passersby inside, even if only to peek at the "famous" stained-glass windows, a gift from some moneybags resident in the early 1900s.

It'd been years since he'd been inside any church, let alone this one, and he had no idea what led him to enter now. Nostalgia, perhaps. A yearning for that time Before, when everything had seemed so much simpler. Or perhaps it was the organ music—practice for midnight Mass, most likely.

Habit steered him to dip his finger in the font of holy water in the vestibule, to cross himself, to at least give a cursory nod toward the altar before slipping into a smooth, wooden pew near the back of the empty church. And indeed, he found the familiarity comforting, even if he was reminded far more of the shenanigans he and his siblings would get up to during Mass than any spiritual revelations he might have had. Inhaling the slightly musty, old church scent, he felt himself relax against the pew's back—as much as he could, anyway—shutting his eyes and letting the music, and the solitude, wash over him.

"Patrick?"

Mildly annoyed at having his peace disturbed, he looked up to see April's cousin Blythe, clearly as surprised to see him as he, her. He forced a smile. "Didn't know you were Catholic."

"I'm not. I was just walking back to my car and the music pulled me in." She smiled "Where's Lilianna?"

"With the family. Having the time of her life."

The tall blonde hesitated, then indicated the empty space beside him. "You mind?"

"So much for churches being sanctuaries," he muttered.

Bizarrely, April's cousin took this as permission to sit beside him, even if a good three or so feet away. Her giant purple purse set by her hip, she tilted her head back, wordlessly taking in the vaulted arches overhead for several seconds before saying, "April's totally wrecked over this, you know."

"Do *not* get on my case, Blythe," he said quietly. "I appreciate how you three gals look out for each other, but you don't know me—"

Her chuckle derailed him. "And what makes you think this is about you, hotshot?" she said, her gaze sharp over a quasi smile. "You're right, I don't know you. Or what really happened—"

"What happened," Patrick said, not as much bitterly as resigned, "is that she got caught up in…the novelty. Until she got a good whiff of reality and realized she couldn't hack it."

"The novelty…? Oh. Because you're her first?"

He leaned forward, the top of the pew grinding into his wrists. "Not sure we should be talking about this in church." Even if, aside from the organist, they were the only two people there.

"I'm sure God's heard worse. And you really think a little hanky-panky's going to blind April to reason? Or turn her into someone she's not?"

Frowning, he twisted around to face April's cousin. "What's that supposed to mean?"

"That underneath all the bubbles, that girl's the most levelheaded person I know. She doesn't do anything on a whim, or without thinking it through, weighing all the options. So there's a reason she picked you. I don't know what that is—and don't care—but I think it's fairly safe to say you can leave the novelty thing out of the equation."

As if, he thought, scrubbing a hand across his jaw. "Fine. That doesn't change the fact that she left. And the only difference between what she did and what my ex did is that

April at least had the decency to end it before Lili could get hurt."

The organ music abruptly ceased, the final chord ghosting around them for several moments before Blythe spoke again. "I assume you know about her family life? And her marriage?"

Having no idea where she was going with this, Patrick nodded.

"Did she tell you the part about her husband offering to release her from their agreement?"

Patrick's head snapped around. "What?"

"Several times, apparently. And each time she refused."

"Why?"

Blythe shrugged. "Because she truly cared about him, for one thing. And for another...she'd made a promise. Yeah, April's *decent* all right. Decent enough to honor her promises, to work her tush off to support her family all those years." She smiled. "Instead of, you know, hanging at the mall and ogling boys like a normal teenage girl." Her hand landed on his arm, the grip firm through his coat. "She doesn't bail on the people that matter to her. Ever."

Patrick slammed his palms onto the pew back, shoved to his feet. "Could've fooled me," he muttered, then started to the far end of the pew.

"You're not getting it, Patrick!" Blythe called behind him. "She didn't leave to save her own butt. She left to save yours!"

Blythe's words reverberated in the vast, empty space, settling around him like volcanic ash. Stopped in his tracks, he wheeled to see her standing as well, her eyes shiny as she hugged her purse to her chest.

"And how do you figure that?" he said.

"How about because I don't think the woman knows *how* to put herself first? Total flaw in her genetic makeup, but whatever. If she had a reason for picking you, then you better believe she had a darn good reason for backing off. And it wasn't about her. But I'm also telling you...give *her* a reason to believe, to *trust* you, and trust *me*—she's yours for life."

Patrick glared at Blythe for several more seconds before continuing to the end of the pew, his head so full he was half surprised it hadn't cracked open. A minute later, however, his skull intact, he found himself back outside, his coat buttoned against the now bitterly cold breeze as he walked the few blocks to his sister's house to get Lili. The crowds had pretty much dispersed; he imagined April was long gone.

The wind pummeled him from what seemed like every direction at once, like a playground bully with ninja powers. Illogically he wanted to rail at it, tell it to leave him the hell alone—

His eyes teared. Because he missed her. Had missed her from the moment she'd walked out his door. And the thing was, he knew Blythe and his mother were both right, that she'd left because he hadn't given her a reason to stay. Hadn't manned up the way she needed him to. And deserved.

But how could he while he was *so damned scared?*

The truth joined forces with the wind to rip the breath from his lungs, nearly deafening him to his phone's ring. His eyes watering, he braced himself long enough to make out the display. His stomach jumped when he did.

"Holy crap, Nat—where the hell have you been—?"

"Sorry, sorry—had to get a new phone, and my internet was down. How's Lili?"

He turned down his sister's street; the wind apparently decided to go knock somebody else around. "Wondering when she's going to see her mother again," he said flatly.

At his ex's silence, he came to a stop and blew out a sigh. "What?"

"I got a job."

"Okay...that's great—"

"In Chicago."

His hand tightened around the phone as the implications sank in. "So Chicago's not that far—"

"They want me to start right away. The day after Christmas."

"But you'll come see Lili before you leave, right?"

Silence. Then: "I don't think that's a good idea, do you? I saw...I know she was upset the last time I was there. I could hear her crying all the way out to my car. And I know you might find this hard to believe, but it tore me up. I can't... it doesn't seem right, to do that to either one of us again."

"Dammit, Nat—"

"Yeah, you go ahead and be as mad as you want, it's not like I don't have it coming. You think I don't know what a lousy wife I was? And a lousier m-mother?" He heard her blow her nose. "I need a fresh start, babe. We all do. Because I can't fix what I broke. And trying to, I feel like I keep making a bigger mess, you know? You—you and Lili—you need to move on. Find somebody who'll be there for you. Forget about me. And she's still young. If I make the break now it won't be so bad, right?"

His hand clamped to his bare head, Patrick spun around, looking at nothing. "Are you freaking *kidding* me? Forget about you? The kid talks about you constantly—"

"Because I keep giving her false hope! Just like my dad did to me all those years. I kept telling myself, at least I saw him sometimes. But you know, all that did was prolong the agony. And I won't do that to Lili. You gotta believe me, Pat—this is for the best."

"So, what? You're gonna pretend your own kid doesn't exist?"

"I didn't say that," Natalie said quietly. "Believe me, I'll think about *her* the rest of my life. And I did love you. But you both…you both need more than I know I'll ever be able to give."

Three, four breath clouds misted in front of his face before he finally said, "You gonna at least let us know where you are?"

"Sure thing," she said, and ended the call. And, in all likelihood, what was left of their relationship.

At this point, the wind could have blown him clean out to sea and he wouldn't have noticed. First Ma, then April's cousin, and now Natalie—holy hell.

It took him the rest of the walk to his sister's to regain his breath. Only to take one look at his baby girl and lose it all over again.

"Ow, Daddy! You're squishing me!"

"Sorry, baby," he said, releasing his daughter from a hug that had probably felt a bit…desperate. Handing him Lili's coat, Frannie frowned.

"What's going on?"

"Noth—" At his sister's glare, he sighed. "I'll call you later, okay?"

"Sure, hon." After Patrick got Lili all bundled up, Frannie reached over to fold him in her arms, her silent support enough, for the moment.

Still wound up, Lili skipped and wiggled and chattered all the way back to their house. And if it was wrong that for once he tuned her out, then sign him up for the Bad Daddy Club. Because while she was going on about seeing Santa and how a-*maz*-ing the boat ride had been, Patrick was trying to catalog all the junk in his brain. Although he knew at least one thing—that there was no way he'd tell Lili about her mother until after Christmas. No point in ruining her holiday for her, and it wasn't like she was going to find out he'd known three days before she did.

The rest of it, though…brother.

Yeah, he'd let April go to save himself the trouble—and pain—of doing it himself later. Because, even more than he had a hard time believing this incredible, loving woman could truly fall in love with him so quickly, he had an even harder time believing that he'd fallen for her.

Like a damn stone.

So he'd fought it. Oh, Lord, had he fought it, with everything he had in him, telling himself it was illogical, and foolish, instead of simply having the grace to accept the damn gift, like his mother had said. To trust that, maybe, just maybe, April was a recompense for everything he'd been through.

And the fear had been his strongest ally, hadn't it? Fear of looking like a failure. A loser. That he'd lose his tenuous grip right in front of April—much worse than he had in the restaurant that night—and there wouldn't be a thing he could do to stop it.

So what?

He flinched.

Yeah, that's right. So you lose it in front of her. You really think that would make a lick of difference to her—?

"Daddy! You're not listening to me!"

"Sorry, baby." Patrick swung her up into his arms for the last block of their walk, smiling when she patted his face with her soft little mittens. "What did you say?"

"That I asked Santa to bring me Mama for Christmas. That was a good thing to ask for, huh?"

Not that Lili's issues hadn't been, and still weren't, valid. Crap—what with everything else that had gone down that night, he'd somehow forgotten about her request. So now what? It was one thing to tell a kid that Santa didn't always bring you what you wanted, if what they wanted was some toy or game or something. But this...

He'd done everything in his power to protect her, to keep her little heart from breaking again so soon. Except he'd set himself an impossible task. In trying to do the impossible, had he quite possibly screwed up a very real chance at happiness?

For both of them?

"Yeah, that was a good thing to ask for," he said softly as he carried her up the stairs and unlocked his front door. Once in the apartment, he hit the switch that turned on the table lamp before setting her down. "But I'm afraid..."

Her eyes were huge. Hopeful. Emotion jammed at the back of Patrick's throat. Sighing, he dropped into the armchair, pulling Lili onto his lap. "Mama's not coming back, baby."

She sat so still Patrick at first wondered if she'd heard him. "How come?" she said, her eyes fixed in his.

"Because she's moving very far away."

"Too far to come see me?"

"Yes."

Her forehead crinkled, Lili started picking at his sleeve. "Never?" she whispered, and Patrick died a little inside.

And the thing was, it wasn't as if he knew for sure that his ex wouldn't change her mind at some point, decide she'd made a mistake, that she wanted to see Lili again. Or at some point down the road even try to patch together something resembling a real relationship with her daughter. Hell, Nat's unpredictability was the only predictable thing about her. But he refused to dangle a carrot in front of his kid.

"*Never* is a very, very long time, baby. I wish I could say I knew for certain what Mama might do, but I can't.

I do know, however, that you're one very lucky kid, having all these people who love you. Me, for one. And then there's Grandma and Poppa and all your aunts and uncles and cousins—"

"But *you* love me most, huh?"

Clearing his throat, Patrick tightened his hold. "Absolutely."

After a moment, Lili wriggled out of his grasp to slide off his lap. Grabbing her Piglet off the sofa, she stuffed her thumb in her mouth and said around it, "Could you turn on the tree?"

That, he could give her.

"Sure thing." He got up to plug in the lights before sitting again, bent forward, waiting for he wasn't sure what. Seconds later Lili reclaimed his lap, wriggling back against his chest to watch the tree. Then she said something he didn't quite get.

"You have to take your thumb out of your mouth, I can't understand—"

"I *said*," Lili repeated as the thumb popped out, "you forgot April."

"What?"

"April." With an exaggerated sigh, she did the palm-up thing. Four going on fourteen, God help him. "You know. *April*. When you talked about all those people who love me? You forgot her. Where is she, anyway?"

His chest tight, Patrick gathered Lili close. "She's been busy," he said over his pounding heart. He reared back to look down at her. "You never talked about her."

"I know."

"Why?"

"Because you didn't," she said with a shrug, and he almost laughed.

"Do you like *her*?"

She gave him a *Well, duh,* look—eye roll and everything—that made him bite his lip. "Of *course*," she said, snuggling back into his arms, and that laugh threatened to erupt, easing the cramp. Guess he could add his kid to the number of females determined to kick his butt in gear that night.

Because *Well, duh,* was right.

Here he'd been so determined to protect his kid, and the kid had things figured out a lot better than he did. *He'd* been the one making things complicated, not Lili. As far as Lili was concerned, he now realized, the hurt over her mother's abandonment and what she felt about April were two separate issues. Like the tares and the wheat, he thought, remembering a bible story from religion class, growing together but not really affecting each other. Lili's bad moods had always been about her mother, never about April. But she couldn't exactly tell him that, could she? Any more than she could explain how she didn't question April's affection or doubt how long it would last. It just was. And God bless her, she was wise enough, and open enough, to simply accept it.

And what kind of example was he setting if he couldn't do the same?

To stop worrying so hard about what *might* happen and simply accept what *was.*

Deciding it was a gold loop earring kind of day, April took her "good" jewelry case out of the small safe in her room and flipped it open, spotting her wedding rings winking at her in the morning sun. The sight of them almost startled her, although she had no idea why. She had even less idea why she pinched them out of their little velvet furrow, slipped them on.

They looked…wrong. As though they belonged to somebody else. Certainly they belonged to another life. She should sell them, she supposed. Not that she needed the money. But she didn't need the rings, either. And as fond as she'd been of Clay, as committed as she'd been to their lives together at the time, when all was said and done they might as well have been part of a costume, like paste jewelry an actor might wear while playing a part.

Not that she was sure what she'd shared with Patrick had been real, either. But what she felt for him was, she thought, breathing through the heaviness still plaguing her as she removed the rings, dropped them back in the box.

Was it strange that she should fall so completely in love in less than a month, when it had taken her longer than that to pick out a paint color for the great room?

She hooked the loops into her ears, thankful that at least she'd been too busy during the day to mope, too exhausted at night to do anything except crash. Or even dream, praise be. Of course, she awakened every morning feeling as though Godzilla was sitting on her chest. And there'd been some sobbing in the shower. Okay, a lot of sobbing in the shower. But then she'd dry herself off, don her big-girl panties and a healthy dose of under-eye concealer, remind herself how goshdarned blessed she was and haul her little butt out to greet her guests, and by the time breakfast was over she could almost convince herself that one day she might even be able to breathe normally again.

Her jewelry case returned to its crypt, April made tracks through the gathering room, exchanging pleasantries with a middle-aged couple sitting on the sunlight-drenched love seat like a pair of cats. The good news was that not only had the inn been full for a week, April could easily have booked twice as many rooms. She'd even given over the room she'd "saved" for her parents, finally accepting that her mother wasn't going to change her mind. Not in this lifetime anyway.

Actually she was coming to terms with the fact that few, if any, humans changed their minds about much, really. At least not any of the humans she knew. In theory, it could happen. In practice, not so much. After all, she could no more change who she was at heart than she could touch the moon.

Meaning, if she cried easily, that's because she felt deeply, and nobody could ever convince her that was a bad thing. Same as nobody could ever make her believe there was such a thing as giving too much. Laughing too much.

Loving too much.

"'Morning, sunshine!" Todd called out as April pushed through the swinging door to the kitchen.

She smiled for her employee, who was switching off mornings with Mel so the poor woman didn't lose her mind—or her husband-to-be. For now they were doing a continental breakfast buffet, mostly dry cereals and pastries and rolls, fruit and yogurt. Except neither Mel nor Todd were averse to whipping up a hot breakfast, if requested.

"Good morning to you, too. So where are we?"

"Coffee's on, juice pitchers are already set up...why don't you take that fruit and bagel platter out, see if anyone wants an omelet? Eggs and bacon? Oatmeal?"

"Got it," April said, laughing. Lord, the man was more of a mother hen than she was.

The large platter firmly clamped in her hands, April nudged open the swinging door to the dining room with her hip and slid sideways into the room, then carted the platter over to the groaning board taking up a good chunk of the back wall. By this time the sunny, coffee-scented room was beginning to fill up with hungry guests, all of whom would be checking out that morning, giving April and the staff a few days' breathing spell before things picked up again after Christmas.

But for now, they were hers to fuss over. And fuss, she did, making the rounds from table to table, greeting everybody by name, asking how they slept, if there was anything they needed, would anyone like a hot breakfast? The room buzzed with conversation, the occasional squawk of a small child, the clinks of flatware against plates. However, unlike every chain hotel in the country, April refused to have a TV in the dining room, figuring if people wanted to plug in to the news that badly, they could check their phones or tablets or whatever.

The toddler squealed again, the sound overloud in what April realized was a sudden dip in the noise level. Her back to the door, she caught a mother clearing her throat, diverting her little boy's attention from whatever he'd been staring at, then shaking her head. April spun around, barely aware that the conversational hiccup had passed.

She couldn't have heard a blessed thing, anyway, what with all the blood rushing in her ears.

Then she saw the look in Patrick's eyes and she could barely see, either, for the tears in hers.

Her silence was unnerving.

Before Patrick began to say he could see April was busy, he'd come back later, that blond-haired giant she'd hired burst out of the kitchen and practically shoved them both outside, declaring he had everything under control. But now, as she led him toward the gazebo, head down and hands shoved into her jacket pockets, Patrick realized he had no idea what he was doing. Or what, exactly, he was going to say. Oh, he knew what he felt, why he was here. It was those damn words that seemed to be eluding him.

And somehow hauling her to him and planting one on her, while it held a definite appeal, didn't feel quite right, either.

So he went for the grovel. Women loved that, right?

"Would it help to admit I've been an idiot?" he finally said to her back as she stomped into the gazebo. April glanced over her shoulder, then climbed up onto one of the bench seats to perch backwards on the railing. The breeze toyed with the fringes of the scarf wound around her neck, black with aqua flecks in it nearly the same color as her eyes.

"I was the one who walked out, remember?"

"I do. But I let you."

She eyed him for a long moment, shivering, although whether from the chill or an attempt to stay in control, he couldn't quite tell. Aching to wrap her in his arms, to show her what he wasn't sure he could say, he took a step closer. But her hand shot up.

"Oh, no, you just stay right where you are—in fact, you could even back up a little, it wouldn't hurt—because it's like your pheromones are sucking out my brain cells. And right now, I need every one of those suckers I can get. Because *damn* it, Patrick…"

Her eyes filled in that way when a man knows to brace himself against the torrent of words to follow. "Walking away that night went against everything I've ever believed about myself. Because I knew you needed me, knew Lili needed me, knew we'd all be good for each other. And… and pretending I could simply toss all that aside felt a whole lot like giving up. Which I don't do."

"I know—"

"I'm not done." She yanked the scarf tighter around her neck. "Except I could tell you were confused, or afraid, or simply not ready, and the last thing I wanted to do was bully you into a revelation. *That's* why I left, not because I didn't care…" A tear slipped out which she smacked away. "But because I did. Do. So you listen up, Patrick Shaughnessy, and you listen up good."

More tears glimmered in her eyes. "I can deal with Lili's moods. Her heartbreak. I ran into your mother, so I know Natalie…" Her lips pressed together, she shook her head. "That sucks, and I'm sorry, but…but more important, nothing *you* can do or think or feel scares me, either. You have nightmares, I'll be there to hold you until they pass. Or panic attacks—I'll be there to talk you down. I'll *be* there, because I *love* you. I love both of you, and I don't give a flying fig whether that messes with your head or not, it just is. Not because you were my first, but because you're my *only*. And, if you didn't want me falling in love with you, you shouldn't've rocked my world the way you did. And I'm not only talking about the sex, although we need to get something straight about that, too. Fine, so maybe I don't have anything to compare it to—which I would think actually works in your favor—but the thing is, after making love with you? Why on *earth* would I want to do it with anybody else? I mean, really?

"So as much as every molecule in my body aches for you, as much as even *thinking* about you touching me gets me halfway to heaven…" She shuddered. "I'm sorry, but it's got to be all or nothing. Because that's what it is for me. But if it isn't for you—" she pointed in the direction of the parking lot "—you can turn right back around and leave."

Patrick's mouth nearly cramped with the effort to not smile, even as his heart cramped for entirely different reasons. And right then, like somebody'd slipped him the answer to the hardest question on the test, he knew what to say.

What to do.

"All or nothing, huh?"

"Yep."

"Well, then…hmm…" He lifted a hand to rub his scarred jaw, then slugged it back in his pocket with a nonchalant shrug. "I guess…I'll just have to ask you to marry me. That *all* enough for you?"

Then he lunged forward to grab her before she toppled backward off the railing. Figured he might as well take advantage of the situation to haul her into his arms. Oddly, she didn't protest, although that might have had something to do with her shock. In fact, she didn't look like she was in any state to protest much of anything, so he whispered, "Can I kiss you now?" and she nodded, so he did. And she wound her arms around him like she couldn't get close enough, laughing and crying at the same time as they kissed, over and over and over, leaving him to wonder how in the hell he'd thought he could let her go.

How he could have refused this gift.

Eventually, however, she planted a hand on his chest and backed up, looking so befuddled it made him want to kiss her all over again. "You c-can't be serious."

Patrick shrugged. "If you're really not going anywhere—"

"No," she said, a smile blossoming across her face.

"Then may as well make it legal. Right? And anyway, Lili told me if I didn't marry you I was a dumbbutt." Because they'd talked some more, that morning over breakfast. You know, just to feel the kid out, make sure he wasn't being presumptuous. Apparently not.

"She didn't."

"She did. And you know I'd do anything for that little girl."

When April laughed, Patrick once more cradled her tear-streaked face, finally and completely and unreservedly accepting the joy shining in her eyes, a joy that finally, and completely, and un-freaking-reservedly sent the last vestiges of fear and doubt packing. "Just like I'd do anything for you," he whispered over the lump in his throat. "Because I love you, too. I *need* you. And swear to God, I always will."

"Oh, Patrick…" April threaded her arms around his waist and pulled him close to lay her cheek against his chest. "Thank you—"

Her cell rang. Patrick held her tighter, *owning* it with everything he had in him. "Ignore it."

"Can't," she said on a sigh, pulling away. "That's Todd's ringtone, he wouldn't be calling unless it was important." She fished her phone out of her pocket, punching it before holding it to her ear. "Hey, what's up?" Then her jaw dropped. "You're kidding? No, no…I'll be right there."

Her phone back in her pocket, April lifted her eyes to Patrick. And damned if she wasn't on the verge of tears *again*. "My parents are here. Ohmigosh, Patrick! My mother…she came! She *came!* I'm so sorry, I've got to go…"

She grabbed his shoulders and gave him a hard kiss, then reared back to slap her temple. "For heaven's sake, what am I *thinking?*"

Clasping his hand, she tugged him down the gazebo steps and back toward the house, clearly intent on introducing him to her parents. Without, he had a strong suspicion, any warning about his existence, let alone his appearance. Or the slightest qualms about the fallout from either. Both. Whether that made her brave or crazy, he had no idea. But it definitely made him even crazier about her.

Halfway across the yard, he swung her around, smiling into her baffled eyes. "Does this mean we have a deal?"

Her grin was brighter than the morning sunshine flickering across the water behind them. "Like to see you try to get out of it, buster," she said, then backed toward the house, pulling him with both hands. Laughing.

And he willingly, joyfully, followed.

Epilogue

Oh, yeah…Santa had outdone himself this year, April thought with a grin as she stretched underneath the comforter in Patrick's bed, squinting at the clock in the predawn light. Another whole hour before she had to be back at the inn.

The comforter shushed over her skin as she rolled onto her stomach to snake her arm across his bare chest. His eyes closed, he smiled, then suddenly shifted to pin her to the bed, making her shriek.

"Happy New Year," he whispered, kissing her neck. She shut her eyes. Melted.

"You said that last night."

He started in on the other side. "'S'worth repeating." Then he lifted his head, his good eyebrow raised. "I can think of something else worth repeating, too."

April looped her hands around his neck. "Telling me you love me?"

"I was thinking more along the lines of showing rather than telling, but yeah. That, too."

She let him continue his nibbling for a moment, then said, "My parents like you."

Who had returned to Richmond a couple days after Christmas. But only after her mother told her how happy she was for her, about her choices. All of them. Not that April had been seeking her mother's approval, exactly, but it was nice to have. Mama clearly still had some heebie-jeebies about being in her mother's house, but she was dealing. And that's all anyone could ask.

Patrick chuckled, his breath teasing that sensitive spot under her ear. "Good to know." Then he rolled to his back and pulled her to his side, entwining his right hand with her left, fingering the darling little ring he'd given her the night before. Something she'd seen and admired in a shop window when, with her parents, they'd taken Lili to Annapolis the day after Christmas.

And yes, her parents adored the little girl, who in turn was thrilled out of her gourd about getting an extra set of grandparents.

April teared up, remembering Patrick's words as he presented the ring the night before—which Lili, who'd spent the night with his parents, had insisted he go all the way back to Annapolis to get.

"Here I was," he'd said, "getting by perfectly okay... and then you came along and showed me I wasn't okay at all. That there was this big, honking hole inside me that I'd figured..." He'd swallowed. "That I figured I may as well get used to being empty. Except you wormed your way inside and filled it, anyway..."

And that had frightened him half to death, he'd said. That he'd get used to the gap being filled, and then she'd leave. Until he'd realized her coming into his life *wasn't a bad thing*. A not-bad thing he should shut up and accept, already.

April still had a hard time dealing with Natalie's decision to sever her connection with him and Lili for good. Thoughts she'd keep to herself, at least for now. The woman had her own issues to work out, none of her concern.

Putting the family back together Nat'd left behind, however?

"Come here," she whispered, smiling when Patrick drew her close again, the obvious happiness in his eyes matching her own as their mouths met.

Mission accepted.

* * * * *

COMING NEXT MONTH from Harlequin
Special Edition®
AVAILABLE JUNE 19, 2012

#2197 THE LAST SINGLE MAVERICK
Montana Mavericks: Back in the Saddle
Christine Rimmer
Steadfastly single cowboy Jason Traub asks Jocelyn Bennings to accompany him to his family reunion to avoid any blind dates his family has planned for him. Little does he know that she's a runaway bride—and that he's about to lose his heart to her!

#2198 THE PRINCESS AND THE OUTLAW
Royal Babies
Leanne Banks
Princess Pippa Devereaux has never defied her family except when it comes to Nic Lafitte. But their feuding families won't be enough to keep these star-crossed lovers apart.

#2199 HIS TEXAS BABY
Men of the West
Stella Bagwell
The relationship of rival horse breeders Kitty Cartwright and Liam Donovan takes a whole new turn when an unplanned pregnancy leads to an unplanned romance.

#2200 A MARRIAGE WORTH FIGHTING FOR
McKinley Medics
Lilian Darcy
The last thing Alicia McKinley expects when she leaves her husband, MJ, is for him to put up a fight for their marriage. What surprises her even more is that she starts falling back in love with him.

#2201 THE CEO'S UNEXPECTED PROPOSAL
Reunion Brides
Karen Rose Smith
High school crushes Dawson Barrett and Mikala Conti are reunited when Dawson asks her to help his traumatized son recover from an accident. When sparks fly and a baby on the way complicates things even more, can this couple make it work?

#2202 LITTLE MATCHMAKERS
Jennifer Greene
Being a single parent is hard, but Garnet Cottrell and Tucker MacKinnon have come up with a "kid-swapping" plan to help give their boys a more well-rounded upbringing. But unbeknownst to their parents the boys have a matchmaking plan of their own.

You can find more information on upcoming Harlequin® titles, free excerpts and more at www.HarlequinInsideRomance.com.

HSECNM0612

REQUEST YOUR FREE BOOKS!

2 FREE NOVELS PLUS 2 FREE GIFTS!

✦ Harlequin®

SPECIAL EDITION

Life, Love & Family

YES! Please send me 2 FREE Harlequin® Special Edition novels and my 2 FREE gifts (gifts are worth about $10). After receiving them, if I don't wish to receive any more books, I can return the shipping statement marked "cancel." If I don't cancel, I will receive 6 brand-new novels every month and be billed just $4.49 per book in the U.S. or $5.24 per book in Canada. That's a saving of at least 14% off the cover price! It's quite a bargain! Shipping and handling is just 50¢ per book in the U.S. and 75¢ per book in Canada.* I understand that accepting the 2 free books and gifts places me under no obligation to buy anything. I can always return a shipment and cancel at any time. Even if I never buy another book, the two free books and gifts are mine to keep forever.

235/335 HDN FEGF

Name _____ (PLEASE PRINT)

Address _____ Apt. #

City _____ State/Prov. _____ Zip/Postal Code

Signature (if under 18, a parent or guardian must sign)

Mail to the **Reader Service:**
IN U.S.A.: P.O. Box 1867, Buffalo, NY 14240-1867
IN CANADA: P.O. Box 609, Fort Erie, Ontario L2A 5X3

Not valid for current subscribers to Harlequin Special Edition books.

Want to try two free books from another line?
Call 1-800-873-8635 or visit www.ReaderService.com.

* Terms and prices subject to change without notice. Prices do not include applicable taxes. Sales tax applicable in N.Y. Canadian residents will be charged applicable taxes. Offer not valid in Quebec. This offer is limited to one order per household. All orders subject to credit approval. Credit or debit balances in a customer's account(s) may be offset by any other outstanding balance owed by or to the customer. Please allow 4 to 6 weeks for delivery. Offer available while quantities last.

Your Privacy—The Reader Service is committed to protecting your privacy. Our Privacy Policy is available online at www.ReaderService.com or upon request from the Reader Service.

We make a portion of our mailing list available to reputable third parties that offer products we believe may interest you. If you prefer that we not exchange your name with third parties, or if you wish to clarify or modify your communication preferences, please visit us at www.ReaderService.com/consumerschoice or write to us at Reader Service Preference Service, P.O. Box 9062, Buffalo, NY 14269. Include your complete name and address.

HSE11B

*The Bowman siblings have avoided Christmas ever since
a family tragedy took the lives of their parents during the
holiday years ago. But twins Trace and Taft Bowman have
gotten past their grief, courtesy of the new women in their
lives. Is it sister Caidy's turn to find love—perhaps with
the new veterinarian in town?*

*Read on for an excerpt from
A COLD CREEK NOEL by USA TODAY
bestselling author RaeAnne Thayne, next in her
ongoing series* THE COWBOYS OF COLD CREEK

***

"For what it's worth, I think the guys around here are
crazy. Even if you did grow up with them."

He might have left things at that, safe and uncomplicated,
except his eyes suddenly shifted to her mouth and he didn't
miss the flare of heat in her gaze. He swore under his
breath, already regretting what he seemed to have no power
to resist, and then he reached for her.

As his mouth settled over hers, warm and firm and tasting
of cocoa, Caidy couldn't quite believe this was happening.

She was being kissed by the sexy new veterinarian,
just a day after thinking him rude and abrasive. For a long
moment she was shocked into immobility, then heat began
to seep through her frozen stupor. Oh. Oh, yes!

How long had it been since she had enjoyed a kiss and
wanted more? She was astounded to realize she couldn't
really remember. As his lips played over hers, she shifted her
neck slightly for a better angle. Her insides seemed to give a
collective shiver. Mmm. This was exactly what two people
ought to be doing at 3:00 a.m. on a cold December day.

He made a low sound in his throat that danced down her spine, and she felt the hard strength of his arms slide around her, pulling her closer. In this moment, nothing else seemed to matter but Ben Caldwell and the wondrous sensations fluttering through her.

Still, this was crazy. Some tiny voice of self-preservation seemed to whisper through her. What was she doing? She had no business kissing someone she barely knew and wasn't even sure she liked yet.

Though it took every last ounce of strength, she managed to slide away from all that delicious heat and move a few inches away from him, trying desperately to catch her breath.

The distance she created between them seemed to drag Ben back to his senses. He stared at her, his eyes looking as dazed as she felt. "That was wrong. I don't know what I was thinking. Your dog is a patient and...I shouldn't have..."

She might have been offended by the dismay in his voice if not for the arousal in his eyes. But his hair was a little rumpled and he had the evening shadow of a beard and all she could think was *yum*.

***

Can Caidy and Ben put their collective pasts behind them and find a brilliant future together?

Find out in A COLD CREEK NOEL, coming in December 2012 from Harlequin Special Edition. And coming in 2013, also from Harlequin Special Edition, look for Ridge's story....

Copyright © 2012 by RaeAnne Thayne

HSEEXP1212

HARLEQUIN®

Desire

ALWAYS POWERFUL, PASSIONATE AND PROVOCATIVE.

**A brand-new Westmoreland novel
from *New York Times* bestselling author**

BRENDA JACKSON

Riley Westmoreland never mixes business with pleasure—until he meets his company's gorgeous new party planner. But when he gets Alpha Blake into bed, he realizes one night will never be enough. That's when her past threatens to end their affair. So Riley does what any Westmoreland male would do…he lets the fun begin.

ONE WINTER'S NIGHT

"Jackson's characters are…hot enough to burn the pages."
—*RT Book Reviews* on *Westmoreland's Way*

Available from Harlequin® Desire December 2012!

www.Harlequin.com

HD73210BJ

When legacy commands, these Greek royals must obey!

Discover a page-turning new Harlequin Presents®
duet from *USA TODAY* bestselling author

Maisey Yates

A ROYAL WORLD APART

Desperate to escape an arranged marriage, Princess
Evangelina has tried every trick in her little black book
to dodge her security guards. But where everyone else
has failed, will her new bodyguard bend her to his
will…and steal her heart?

Available November 13, 2012.

AT HIS MAJESTY'S REQUEST

Prince Stavros Drakos rules his country like his
business—with a will of iron! And when duty demands
an heir, this resolute bachelor will turn his sole
focus to the task….

But will he finally have met his match in a world-
renowned matchmaker?

Coming December 18, 2012,
wherever books are sold.

www.Harlequin.com

HP13109